Ilaria

or

The Conquest of Disobedience

GABRIELLA ZALAPÌ

Translated from the French with an Afterword by Adriana Hunter

Linden Editions

Linden Editions, 110 Standen Rd, London SW18 5TS
www.lindeneditions.com

Originally published in French as *Ilaria ou la conquête de la désobéissance* in 2024 by Éditions Zoé

This translation first published in the USA in 2025 by Other Press
First published in the UK in 2026 by Linden Editions

9 8 7 6 5 4 3 2 1

ISBN: 978-1-9191960-0-8
eISBN: 978-1-9191960-1-5

A CIP catalogue record for this book is available from the British Library

Cover image © Maria Norek
Cover design © Tasja Puławska

Offset by Tetragon, London
Printed in England by CMP (UK) Ltd.

EU Authorised Representative: Easy Access System Europe – Mustamäe tee 50 10621 Tallinn, Estonia, gpsr.requests@easproject.com

MAY 1980

Aged eight, I like the sensation of my upper body dangling free, the contact of my knees hooked over metal. I like the moment when I close my eyes tight, let go of the bar with my hands, and feel the giddiness thrill through me. When my hands are flat on the black asphalt, that means I've overcome my fear. And that's when I picture my favorite gymnast, Nadia Comăneci. She has her arms spread wide. Victory.

I adopt this hanging position whenever we have recess or I'm waiting for Ana, my sister. When she left me this morning she said, See you back here *on time,* okay? Or I'll go home alone. "Here" is at the foot of the steps, near the metal rail that separates the parking lot from the schoolyard.

Ilaria! Get down from there! We're going to Chez Léon. Come on, move it!

I recognize Dad's voice. Surprised, I lift the bottom of my dress that's blocking my view. Those are definitely the tips of his shoes, that's definitely his impatient voice. I swivel around the bar, land on my feet, and smooth down my dress.

Ana's about to show up.

No, no. Change of plan. Mom's picking her up from school and we're meeting at Chez Léon. Come on!

I take his hand, it's clammy.

Since our parents separated and Dad moved to Turin, we meet at a restaurant once a month. It was Mom who came up with the idea. She prefers neutral territory. She says they fight too much at home. And it's true, they do hold back at Chez Léon. Even if Dad does clench his jaw and Mom stares into space, pretending not to care.
No, Dad still hasn't found a job. When he says "Nope-no-work" his voice is always sad, tired. Mom turns away slightly to hide her smile and Dad gets mad. He uses the word "humiliation" a lot. Luckily, the waiter comes over and puts down plates of perch fillet or bowls of meringue with whipped cream. Thanks.

After dessert, Ana and I get up from the table and go out to the small beach where we choose pebbles. We practice skipping stones.

Did you see?
What?
Dad took Mom's hand.

To get to Chez Léon we go through the village of Hermance, cross the French-Swiss border, and keep going along the road to Yvoire. Dad has a navy blue BMW, a 320 coupe.
Tell me if you see a phone booth. He lights a cigarette. There! He stops, gets out, and produces some coins from his pants pocket. His back pressed to the glass, the creases

in his shirt making *v* and *w* shapes. I wait, lower my window to let in some air. The leather seat no longer burns the backs of my thighs, it even feels soft when I stroke it.

Inside the phone booth, Dad's talking loudly. He raises his voice some more and turns around. His eyes meet mine. I can tell he's upset from the way he's moving his hands. He's bolt upright. That's worrying.
When he comes back, he says Mom changed her mind and doesn't have time for lunch. We're going to spend the weekend together. What about school? You can skip school for just a few days... It's not that big of a deal.

Dad's voice is sharp. I count on my fingers: Thursday, Friday, Saturday, Sunday. Four days. What about Ana? I want to protest, but when Dad's cranky it's best not to say anything.

He starts up the car with a lurch and stabs out his cigarette. His forehead is covered in sweat.

Mont Blanc Tunnel, French-Italian border, arched ceilings in the tunnels, hairpin bends in the Valle d'Aosta, carsickness. We stop under a sky weighed down by a layer of gray. The landscape is metallic. I throw up by the side of the road and Dad hands me a white cotton handkerchief. Let's go get a drink, it'll do you good. A few kilometers farther down the mountainside, in the gas station's bar, Dad's face is pale. It must be the neon lights. He pays the woman at the checkout for two slices of Margherita pizza, a whiskey, a coffee, and a lemonade. I hate lemonade but don't say anything, my mouth is dry.

Do you sell tokens for the phone?
How many?
Maybe twenty.
The checkout assistant carefully counts out the yellowish tokens and hands them to Dad.
The booth is outside, on the left.
Her nails are very long and covered in very red varnish. I follow Dad.

What are those tokens?
I need them to make calls. You can't put actual money in phone booths in Italy.

Between Geneva and Turin, Dad makes several calls. Five in all. Whenever he sees a gas station he stops. Are you glad you're spending the weekend with me? Did you lose your tongue? What are you thinking about?

Nothing.

Turin. We drive around for a long time looking for somewhere to park and when Dad nudges open the door to his building with his shoulder, he looks relieved. I launch myself up the stairs. What floor is it? The fourth. Up on his landing, he looks for his keys. You're going to see your bedroom. Are you happy? I say yes. Yes, I'm happy. Listen, Ilaria, he turns the key in the lock, I need to introduce you to someone I haven't yet mentioned, her name's Geneviève. Who is she? The lady of the house. Dad opens up and points at a lifeless dummy in a black dress with a white lace collar and a hat. He roars with laughter. Geneviève's face is made of white polystyrene, with no eyes. Go on! In you go. Your room's down at the end, past the bathroom.
Impatient to see it, I glance quickly at the other rooms, then turn on the light in my bedroom. The space is crammed with two beds and two chests of drawers. I go over to a *Topolino* poster. Mickey Mouse looks at me with his tunnel eyes. Dad is hanging back in the doorway.

I haven't yet found any pretty bedside lamps. We could buy some together tomorrow, couldn't we? If you like. I run my hand over the fabric and ask if these are the sheets we had in Florence.
Do you remember it?
I think so, yes. When was Florence?
Two years ago.

The orangey sunflower shapes jump out at me from the sheets. They bring back the hazy images I still have of those days. Two years but it feels like centuries ago that Mom, Ana, and I moved to Switzerland.

We wake early the next day and head out for *un giro,* a car trip around Turin. Dad tells me all about the FIAT kingdom, the workers' strikes, the influx of immigrants from the south. He says the locals hate them.
He points things out through the windshield, the palazzi, the River Po, the Basilica of Superga, statues. You see those kids in between the cars over there, they're *posteggiatori.* That's how they make money, helping people park.

When we walk under the arches along the Corso Vittorio Emanuele II, Dad holds my hand firmly. His is still clammy and I don't dare pull mine away until we're outside the Al Sogno toy store, then I let go.
The window display looks like a zoo of harmless animals. Even the snakes look friendly. Dad checks out where I'm looking. Did that teddy bear catch your eye? Come, we'll buy him. The store is full of wooden toys, mobiles, and dolls in sparkly dresses. I'm dazzled. What about Ana? What should we get for her? Yes, a doll...Ana loves them. The one I choose has very long eyelashes and she closes her eyes when she lies down. While we wait for the sales assistant to gift wrap her in fancy paper, Dad hands me the teddy bear. What shall we call him? How about Birillo? Yes. I look at Birillo and instantly adopt his shiny,

milk-chocolate-colored eyes, his creamy belly and soft fur. Dad pinches my cheek between his first two fingers with a soppy look in his eyes.

That pinch of my cheek is like his signature. He'll keep doing it for two whole years and I'll end up hating it.

Are you happy?

Aged eight, I'm quiet, submissive, kind of skinny. I don't complain when Dad leaves me on my own in the apartment to go make phone calls at Carmelo's, the bar downstairs. He doesn't have his own phone. I'll be back real soon. He always promises he'll be "two minutes." Left alone, lying on my bed, I draw or put Sarah Kay figurine stickers into my new sticker book. Dad bought it for me at the kiosk. And when I'm bored of waiting for him, I know where to find him: at the bar. My landmark is the big coffee machine that gives off this smell of burned caramel.

Workmen from the neighborhood come to Carmelo's for a sandwich at lunchtime or a drink before heading home. They all go by their first names and always order the same thing. *Una birra alla spina per Emilio e due tramezzini per Marco*. Gianna runs the place. She punches down the big keys on the register so quickly. *Sei mila lire*. Perched on her little podium, she smiles, hands out packs of cigarettes and the *scontrini*, the receipts. When the place is empty, she sweeps the floor. Carmelo himself wipes the counter, serves coffees, dries glasses with a cloth, and levels out the sugar in the sugar casters.

When I walk into the café the place is buzzing. The workmen are all singing along to a song on the radio. *Vorrei essere libero, libero come un uomo.* I wend my way through them to reach the bar and haul myself onto a high stool. Listen, listen! It's a Giorgio Gaber song, "La libertà." Carmelo laughs and I can see flashes of metal at the back of his mouth. How many fillings? I don't have time to count them. Are you looking for Fulvio? He points toward the phone booth with a hand covered in soap suds.

Dad appears later. His legs are very stiff. He has a weird look on his face and leans toward my ear. We're leaving this evening. His breath feels like a draft. Hurry. We need to go pack our bags.
Say goodbye and thank you to Carmelo and Gianna *like a good girl.*

I'm in the backseat of the car, having trouble breathing. Where are we going? To the seaside. What about Ana? And Mom? When are we meeting up with them? Stop sniffing. We're going back to Geneva in a month. A month isn't long. What about the end-of-year party? You said we were just spending the weekend together... You can go next year. Enough already with the questions.
I can picture the pretty dress I chose with Mom for the parade. I think about Sarah, my best friend, about my teacher and the little flag we made in class, and Ana. My head feels heavy. I bend my legs and bring my knees up under my chin, and hug Birillo close. I fall into a cold, restless sleep.

I want to hear your voice STOP The kid is fine STOP She wants to talk to you STOP I'm waiting for you STOP Wait for me STOP
Your husband

Here! Put that in the glove compartment.
Now we don't pull over just at phone booths but at post offices too. Dad sends a whole bunch of telegrams and keeps copies of them. I don't dare read them when he passes them to me, but being curious, I handle them slowly so I can catch a few words.

Zzaaack, zzzaaack. A family, a lone man, a woman. Two mops of white hair going along at thirty kilometers an hour in the right-hand lane. Dad's losing his patience, he lets go of the steering wheel and lights a cigarette. Come on!!! Let me through. He slaloms between the vehicles. Are you scared? A little. He notices my hand clinging tightly to the door handle. The traffic heading into Genoa is heavy, there are lots of tunnels. Shade-light, shade-light. The lanes are clogged with cars and long trucks. I can't take any more of this road. Get the map, Ilaria.

Genoa, Milan, Brescia, Alessandria. Yes, Brescia, then we'll go to Alessandria. I follow our route with the tip of my finger. But there's no seaside at Alessandria! That doesn't matter. I'm showing you around your country. Dad says this playfully. He's very close to winking at me.
He downshifts and takes the exit lane for the gas station.

I need to make a call, go to the bar.
No, I'm staying here.

While I wait for him, I hop around the phone booth. Dad feeds tokens into the slot on the phone and lights a cigarette. *Pronto?* The conversation goes on and on.
I sit in the car with the door open, swinging my legs. The sky's filled with trails of white, the clouds are like balls of wool. It's muggy, I'm thirsty and hot. Other cars come, then leave, reversing in the parking lot. Kids run around. Watch out, look before you cross! their mothers cry. The families that pass me look perfect, washed, combed, ironed, heading somewhere specific. Where are we going?

Roads, phone booths, post offices, small hotels, bars. The days are racking up. We often stop at Autogrill roadside restaurants to get gas, eat sandwiches, and use the restrooms. I like them. Everything inside is colorful: the piles of candy, the baskets of food wrapped in squeaky paper, the tubs of music cassettes, the games, the plushies. And while I roam around the aisles, Dad chats with customers at the bar.
He loves to talk.
He can't help himself, he has to talk to someone. Anyone. And he's very good at striking up a conversation. It always starts with a comment about the traffic or the weather, or with a joke. Dad can make even the shiest people feel comfortable. He looks so at home, it's the way he leans on the bar, how he speaks to the bartender. When he clowns around he's soon surrounded by smiling faces. I like it better when he's like that, happy with a cheerful twinkle in his eye, instead of having to listen to his theories about people.

Yes, yes, we're leaving. Always one last slurp. He drinks very quickly and when he snatches up his glass, I'm convinced that he'd be just as sure of himself if he were blind. His lips would quiver in exactly the same way. It's like he's scared he won't have time to finish his whiskey.
He once told me it was a medication for him, and he pinched my cheek.
Say thank you. I thank the bartender, say goodbye to the others individually.

On the road again. That's how we leave these bars, abruptly. The show's over, thank you and goodbye.

Vroom, vroom.

What do you want to eat?
I don't know.
You don't eat anything.
Where are we going next?
Maybe Trieste. I don't know yet. We'll find somewhere.
Are we staying in a hotel?

I don't like sleeping in rooms over small-town bars. I don't know if it's the cold, impersonal bedrooms that I hate most or the never-ending evenings in the bars themselves. I sit at the bar half listening to what Dad's describing—his exploits at horse shows, his adventures as a young soldier. And I don't understand anything he says about politics.

Sitting there with my elbows on the zinc countertop, I prefer watching the other customers, the ones playing cards or the slightly isolated ones staring sadly into the mirror behind the bottles. What are they thinking about? Are they shy? I make up tons of stories. I think that maybe this guy's alone because he had a fight with his wife. Or that one's sad because his dog died. I'm scared of making eye contact with them, but I still want them to know that I see them, that we're part of the same family, the silent ones. When it does happen, I look away, jump down from the stool, and go slip some coins into the jukebox or play pinball. Dad gives me as many coins as I like, especially so long as I leave him in peace.

Bang, boom, bing. I've gotten skilled with these colorful balls shut inside their brightly lit box.

Another game. One last one.
These games delay the moment when he sends me off to bed.
I don't like the bedrooms. I feel lonely in them. The barmen always say they're just there to help people out of a tight spot. The beds have saggy mattresses. Before picking a bed, I jump on them and choose the less wrecked one. The floor tiles are cold, the sheets questionable. Once I'm upstairs, I don't waste any time, I brush my teeth and go to bed, with Birillo tight against my stomach. I wait for sleep, listen for Dad's footsteps, for when he comes through the door and collapses onto his bed fully clothed. After just a few seconds his breathing gets heavy. He's fast asleep. The world no longer exists. A smell of tobacco and alcohol in the air. I open the window, untie his shoelaces, take off his shoes, peel off his socks, and put a glass of water on the nightstand. Dad always goes to sleep on his back with his hands crossed over his chest. I get back into my own bed. My body perched on the edge of the mattress. I fall asleep like that, on the brink of a precipice.

We leave these rooms early in the morning. Coffee. Brioche. *Spremuta d'arancia* for me.
We only skim through, dip briefly into people's lives.
We leave no trace, maybe a few memories for the customers the night before.
Once we're settled in the car, Dad turns on the radio.
I've stopped asking, Where are we going?

The radio announcer says: *The weather for July 19. Unsettled conditions are expected over central Italy in the next twenty-four hours. This bad weather has come up from Tunisia and is moving toward Eastern Europe. It will be followed by better conditions.*

Passing on your daughter's disappointment for not talking to you STOP I reject all accusations of abduction STOP *Le bugie hanno le gambe corte* Lies have short legs STOP Do you think you'll get far like this STOP

We live in profile, Dad and me. I know the outline of his nose really well, the oval shape of his ears, the hairs that stick out from his eyebrows, just above his glasses frame. I can even identify his mood from the way he sighs and groans and moves. When he gnaws the thick skin around his thumbnail that means he's thinking and will soon want to make *una telefonata*. If we're a long way from a gas station, he'll smoke to wait it out. He'll open a soft pack of cigarettes by catching the tab between his lips and pulling it. He'll use his index finger to force a gap in the silvery paper and then tap-tap the pack against the steering wheel to get a cigarette out.

How many phone calls since we left? Hundreds. How many days has it been?

The next exit is in three kilometers. Dad points to the sign by the side of the road. We'll fill up with gas too.

Phone booths are cages on the frontier between three worlds. When Dad starts talking, I see all three dancing around inside that little box: Mom's world, Dad's world, and the world of the freeway. Even if I can't hear what he's saying, I get the feeling he's playing ping-pong. His words go flying, bouncing off the glass walls. Cigarette, cigarette, cigarette. There's smoke everywhere. Dad opens the door, wedges it with his right foot, slips tokens into the slot. When he's in this comical position, his body morphs. His neck gets stiff, red, and swollen, his hands shake. He does this nervous laugh. He gesticulates, points his finger in the

air. It's going to go on for hours still and he'll come back in a terrible mood.
Before he puts the phone down, I hear Dad cry, Don't hang up!
I breathe once, twice, then hold my breath.
I make myself as small as possible.

I'll put you on with Mom next time.

When someone asks Dad where we're going, he names a town on the other side of Italy. When they ask what his job is, he says entrepreneur, engineer, lawyer... A real one-man band who can speak every occupation, every language, every jargon. Lying comes naturally to Dad, he does it very politely, with his eyes. He gives a whole bunch of details as if describing a picture. He's so good at it and is so precise that everyone believes him.
But all his lies can't change the growing silence between us. A real can of worms.

Why do you invent all that stuff?
What's it to them where I live and what I do? I'm with you, that's what matters. Dad tries to catch my eye, I look away. Don't worry about the lies. They're nothing, nothing at all. Come on! Turn on the radio.

The announcer: *Edizione straordinaria. Today, July 23, 1980, the magistrate Mario Amato was assassinated at eight o'clock in the morning while waiting for a bus on the Viale Jonio in Rome. He was shot in the back of the neck. The assassin fled the scene on a powerful motorbike driven by his accomplice.*
Mario Amato was conducting an inquiry into far-right gangs spreading terror in the capital. He had discovered links between state institutions and neo-fascist youth groups. With his last words he said that the country is on the brink of civil war.

Before we go into an Autogrill, Dad always straightens his tie and jacket, then proceeds confidently. He says you should be elegant when traveling. Next to him, I feel like a bundle of hair poking out in every direction. Things improve slightly with my skirt. It's like an upside-down tulip. I've been wearing it since we left and when I point this out to Dad, he says we're not far from Florence and yes, I need some clothes. Perfect timing.

An hour later we're at Standa, a large store. The children's department is on the second floor. Neon lights, advertising announcements, escalators. Dad grumbles. I hate these places, pick what you want, but be quick about it.
I go around in circles. It's usually Mom who buys my clothes.
What size are you?
I don't know.
Dad is losing his patience and ends up talking to a sales assistant. He thinks she's pretty, I can tell. He smiles and goes all sappy. His voice changes too. Ilaria needs everything, including a swimsuit. I'll let you decide! Then to me, I'm leaving you with this very nice lady. I'm going to make *una telefonata* then I'll be back.

The assistant crouches down. My name's Livia. And you're Ilaria? What would you like? Do you know what size you are? My brain scrambles. What's your favorite color? She speaks softly as she shows me dresses, pants, socks, and underwear. Yes, I like them.

An hour goes by. I'm sitting next to the checkout with my eyes pinned on the escalator. When Dad finally appears, he laughs. I wasn't going to abandon you here. Look what I found. With a big smile, he hands me a Piero Ciampi cassette.

Back at the wheel of the car he listens intently to the singer, each note on the piano, the violins. Every evening, I go back to the place where you squeezed my hand. Your face is an evening full of shadows. *Torno ogni sera dove tu stringevi la mia mano. Ed il tuo viso è una sera piena di ombre.*
Dad has stopped talking. When I turn to him, his cheeks are shiny, they're covered in tears. I wish I could comfort him, but I don't know how. So I put my hand on his arm. He smiles at me. My princess... well, *you* understand me. It's the first time he's called me "my princess."

Light me a cigarette. My hands are shaking too much.
I object.
Don't make such a fuss, come on! Take out a cigarette and when you bring the lighter flame up close, breathe in. It's easy, give it a try.
I reluctantly do as I'm told. Surprised by the acrid smoke in my throat, I cough.
You're all red! Dad laughs.

Clutching Birillo, I watch Dad's reflection in the bathroom mirror.

Dad is armed with his shaving brush, daubing his cheeks with a thick layer of soap. As the razor passes, the white foam gradually reveals his smooth skin. The tracks are wide, clear-cut. He concentrates, twists his mouth, pulls his nose forward when he focuses on his chin. His hands move confidently, cautiously around his neck. Then he turns the tap and lets the water pool in his cupped palms. He splashes his face, erasing every trace of foam, and towels down his cheeks, forearms, and elbows. He takes out his bottle of eau de cologne and dabs a few drops on his neck.

As he returns from the phone booth, Dad says *Avanti!* It's like the word gives him the strength, the will to keep driving. He presses his foot down on the accelerator, making the engine roar, grips the steering wheel, and slaloms. He says we're *indivisibili*. The greatest, my princess ... the greatest. There's something final about the way he says it. I cling to the door handle and think about the word *indivisibili*. All those *i*'s wandering about on our flying saucer.

With his eyes locked onto the road, Dad asks what time it is. Two o'clock. Turn on the radio.

Tellegiornale delle ore quattordici. Edizione straordinaria. An explosion has damaged the whole right side of the train station in Bologna. Fifty-five people have been killed and eighty injured, several of them seriously. The cause of the tragedy has not yet been determined. The most plausible hypothesis is that a water heater in the second-class waiting room exploded, but more than three hours after the incident, an anonymous telephone call claimed that it was a bomb attack carried out by the far-right movement the NAR, the Armed Revolutionary Nuclei.

My God! Fifty-five dead, Dad says under his breath.
A long silence. We should avoid major roads, there'll be police roadblocks everywhere. That's not great for us.
Why not?
Your mother's looking for us. It would just take one overenthusiastic police officer and I'll end up in prison. You don't want me to go to prison, right?

My throat tightens.
Mom's looking for us?
No, I'm kidding, my princess. Everything's fine. Get the map.

I hesitate, then take the map from the glove compartment and open it out. Dad points to a road. I was thinking of going along here, see? It's the Autostrada del Sole. Look, it goes from Milan to Naples, 760 kilometers of concrete, bridges, and viaducts. That freeway changed the face of Italy. A total revolution. "We must develop the country." I still remember Moro saying that on television.
Look, can you see, here, Bologna, Siena, Orvieto, Monte Cassino, Naples . . . ? We're changing our route. We'll go that way.

Dad's never short of ideas when he needs to come up with a solution. I open the window, lean my head out, and watch the landscape scroll by. The azure of the sky is almost blinding. The air is dry. I swallow my saliva.

Are you bored? Do you want to learn to drive? I shrug. He takes a country road and when he stops, tells me to sit on his lap and put my hands over his.
Hold the steering wheel tight! I squeeze my fingers around it and look straight ahead. He starts up the engine and eases forward. Then accelerates. I laugh. I'm scared. I laugh because I'm scared. It's up to you to change gears, listen to the engine. We spend several hours on that country road. Holding the steering wheel, changing gears, avoiding potholes.

Fear, laughter. One way, then back. One way, then back. Do you like it? Then he stops and opens the hood. A car is also its engine. Dad launches into very complicated explanations. Each thing plays its part. He touches, unscrews, rescrews. His white handkerchief is covered in engine grease, but he's proud of himself. Proud to ask me questions and especially proud of my answers.

Your phone is working fine STOP Why break off contact STOP The father of your children STOP

The sun's been blinding us for hours on the road. It's been a long day because Dad decided to take minor roads. He says there are loads of policemen on the freeway. They're looking for terrorists.
He points at the horizon. Over there is Yugoslavia and that is the Adriatic Sea.
Just a little bit longer, Ilaria. We'll soon be in San Benedetto.
But we stop before that.

The expanse of water is there at the end of a steep track that opens onto a long yellow beach. Two blue lines in front of us—the sky and the sea. I'd stopped believing we'd see it.
Dad brings the car to a halt, he's very excited. He takes off his shoes, flings aside his socks, folds the hem of his pants up to his knees, and runs over the sand to the waterline. When he turns around, he's all lit up by a smile. And when he runs, he hardly touches the sand. His feet are as light as air. He wants me to join him. Come here! Come! It's fantastic. The sand's hot.

The start of ten days of vacation. Ten days of vacation after two months of driving. Ten days against a backdrop of turquoise. Ten days under a red-and-white-striped parasol. Ten days of such heat that Dad's return trips to the phone booth and the post office grow less frequent. Ten days of drowsiness, waves, splashing, kids yelling, Pass me the ball, on the beach. Ten days of an orange rubber ring shaped like a duck, of sandcastles and silence you could cut with a knife.
Don't you want to play with the other kids?

No.
Don't you want to swim?
Yes. "Yes" to make him happy. I know Dad's watching me and thinks I'm a bad swimmer. You should do it like this. His frog actions sitting on his deck chair don't help me at all but they make the beach-neighbors he's been chatting with laugh.

One afternoon he takes me over to the rocks. Jump! Jump or I'll push you, you don't have a choice. The rock is scorching under my feet. I hesitate. Take a step forward. I think of Nadia Comăneci. I picture the concentration on her face, her bangs that stop above her eyebrows, her muscly legs on the beam. She starts her sequence, her leaps and splits. Her feet are always raised in demi-pointe. Her white leotard makes her look like an angel. I picture her doing one last backward somersault and landing on the mat, upright, arms wide, forming a *v*. Victory.
I jump.

Under the water everything stops. When I open my eyes, I'm in a liquid sky. I want to stay there, invisible, suspended in this peacefulness. But I need air. I draw water into my nostrils. Nadia reappears with her *v* for victory. I absolutely have to get back to the surface. Dad greets me with a roar of laughter. Bravo, my princess!

We're staying at Nino's, a hotel-bar-restaurant on the main square. During the day our room's really like an oven, but in the evenings the balcony's perfect with its soft breeze. From there we can watch people strolling along the Corso. There's a relaxed, festive atmosphere and I wonder if Dad would rather be at the bar than here with me. But I don't say anything. I don't want to spend hours waiting for him. Children run in every direction and have fun splashing themselves with water from the fountain. Their parents chat. Teenage boys glued to their Vespas pretend not to notice passing girls, but then laugh as soon as the girls have their backs turned. Old people sit on benches. They watch everything, without a word, as if they're at the theater.

You can feel it in the air, the end of the vacation is on its way.

With his chin resting on the balustrade Dad glances at me.

Shame Mom and Ana aren't here with us.

Yes, it's a shame. When are we going home?

He clears his throat, takes a loud deep breath, and glances at me again.

You know, your mom and me... love each other. But we don't understand each other, she says I don't let her live. I don't know how to do that. Life with her's become impossible. You remember how her mood changes? How she's always changing her mind? One evening it'll be yes, the next morning it's no. First we're meeting at a restaurant, then it's, Oh, actually we're not. With no explanation. I thought it over... right? She always says *I thought it over.* She says she's tired, she's doing the work of two people, she has to take care of everything at home, and she can't

take any more. She's changed so, so much since you've been living in Geneva. Life was straightforward before.
Before what?
Before you two were born. We did everything together, absolutely everything. We were stuck to each other. We couldn't survive for one minute without each other. Your mother's gotten so serious since you've been around. She says she can't stand me anymore.
Dad thumps the balustrade, and it makes me jump. It feels like I put my fingers in an electrical socket. He's talking very angrily. In profile, the muscles of his clamped jaws are bunched into balls. He goes into the bedroom and starts pacing up and down. Like a stressed leopard. He's staring down at the floor tiles but everything about his surroundings has disappeared. He brings the bottle of whiskey to his lips and takes a long slug. Gluglug, gluglug.

I mean just think, Ilaria, it happened overnight... when I got back to Florence the apartment was empty. Completely empty.
No Mom, no nothing.
Not even a note, an explanation. Nothing. She ran away with you girls under her arms. It was a shock for me, that's only natural, surely? My life evaporated just like that. In a trice. Do *you* think that's fair? I'm picturing Mom closing the living-room door and asking Dad to stop shouting. Sometimes she'd give us the Ping-Pong paddles and tell us to go out for a while.

Dad takes a deep breath, once twice three times.

I just wish we could love each other like before. We were happy before. And now what? I live on my own in Turin. In that horrible city. I try to understand your mother, I do everything I can to please her, but I don't want to take on just any job! She says she wants a divorce and doesn't love me anymore... She's lying. I'll never sign the divorce papers. I need to make her change her mind.
Dad's breathing hard. He's holding back words that explode inside his mouth. No way he can chew them. He doesn't say anything for a long time.
How dare she think our love is over? Your mother's always been a filthy liar! She's unstable. What does she think? That I'll just obey her?

He sits down on the bed, puts his head in his hands, crosses his fingers over the back of his neck, and, after a long silence, turns to me.
Do you miss Mom? And Ana?
His voice is gentle now. I shrug.
He peers at me, amazed.
Well, *I* miss Mom a lot.

I wonder whether we're talking about the same person.

Resting on one elbow, Dad chain smokes. It's hot enough to shatter rock. We have the windows wide open and the wind blasts into the car. I turn up the volume so I can hear the music. The cassettes are playing flat out. Side A, side B. The song lyrics get embedded in my head. I know Ornella Vanoni's by heart and the ones from "L'Appuntamento." That song reminds me of Mom, the way she used to hum along to it, replacing the words with Mmm Mmmms. But she always made up for it in the chorus, which she knew by heart. *Amore è già tardi e non resisto. Se tu non arrivi non esisto. Non esisto, non esisto.* It's late, my love, and this waiting I can't resist. If you don't come back, I don't exist, I don't exist.
I often rewind, several times over.

I'm hungry, Dad.

In the distance, the bridge at the Cantagallo Autogrill sketches superfine lines over the freeway. It looks like an insect, a spider with just two legs seen in profile. We choose a table in the second-floor restaurant. Dad watches cars go by through the huge window. Where the hell are all those people going? It feels like being on a boat, huh? Ugh, a sea of concrete . . . And to think this gas station was opened by the Archbishop of Bologna! In his speech he said this road was like the one from Galilea to Jerusalem . . . Pfff. The garbage we have to listen to!

He toys with his cold food with the end of his fork, then pushes his plate away and orders another whiskey. His face relaxes. I eat a little while he looks over his shoulder, settles his glasses on the bridge of his nose, and lights a cigarette. A woman walks past, Dad watches her. The waiter comes over. Another whiskey, another whiskey, another whiskey.

Where are we sleeping tonight? In an hour he'll say he needs a nap, unless something else—the traffic, the smell of fresh tarmac, the bucket of a digger, or roadwork—makes us switch to another road.

Dad likes driving and sometimes he prolongs the pleasure as late as possible into the night. Cocooned in darkness, we listen to "My Funny Valentine." Dad loves that song. He loves jazz. He says you have to listen to it at night, you can hear the notes better.

That man must be very lonely, says Dad, lighting a cigarette. And sad. Can you hear the loneliness, Ilaria?

The voice makes me think of talcum powder, of velvet, and when I look up ahead, the fabric of it swallows everything except the majestic black trees standing tall by the side of the road. It consumes everything, including my memories. The farther we get from Geneva, the more it feels like I'm walking down a corridor with my eyes closed.

I think about the words I no longer hear, "Go tidy your room," "Go brush your teeth," "Come, it's dinnertime." These little phrases bind me to home, to my life before. I try to picture the route to school, my desk in the classroom, I try to conjure the smell of the soap at home, the layout of the furniture in my bedroom, but something's stopping me. I obstinately invent details to fight off the doubt creeping over me: Does Geneva exist?

We're safe from everything here, Ilaria. Right? Do you like nighttime?

What are you thinking about, Ilaria?

Go ahead! Go! Go stretch your legs.
We're at a playground, Dad sits himself on a bench and turns up the collar of his jacket. The temperature's changing, it's chilly this morning. Swing, merry-go-round, then I join him again.
Smell this! I bring my hand to his face so he can catch the smell of rusted metal on my palm.
Don't ever do that again. He says it harshly. Releases my wrist.

I take a few steps back. Two days ago he rubbed his hands on tree trunks, it smells of wood, on pebbles, it smells of stone, on metal, it smells of rust. We had a lot of fun.

I return to the swing, my back turned to Dad. A girl comes over. You want to play off-ground tag with us?
Some other kids a little way away are waiting for my answer. I hesitate, wipe away my tears. Okay.
I jump, straddle various obstacles, and show off my specialty: hanging upside down. I'm no longer scared of dangling there with my arms free.

Do you live in Florence?
No.
Where then?
The children's eyes study me intently and I don't know what to say. I feel like pointing at the car but stop myself.
I live in Switzerland. How about you?
We live in Taranto. What grade are you in?

Come on, kids! We're leaving! Their parents want to hit the road again. I watch them walk away.
What about me, am I not going back to school?
Dad looks at the end of his cigarette, takes a long drag on it, and holds his breath.
You know, Ilaria, right now there are more important things. Mom and I have decided that you'll stay with me a bit longer. The smoke comes out of his mouth in little bursts. Do you understand?

I don't dare say no, I don't dare say I don't understand, and I couldn't care less about more important things. I want to go to school, I want to play, see my friends, go to birthday parties, to gym class. I want to do handsprings and rolls, train on the beam and be like Nadia Comăneci. I want to go home. Then the idea of not being with Dad makes me freeze. I can't leave him on his own. I look closely at him, sit down next to him, rest my head on his shoulder, and slip my hand through his elbow. He strokes my cheek and pinches it. What's gotten into you, my little princess?

What does CR mean? Cremona. And FR? Frosinone. Car number plates are like riddles. Then we play yellow car and red truck.
In the distance, wooded hills, open plains, and abandoned warehouses. The electric wires from metal poles remind me of the pictures I drew when I was younger: a horizontal line for arms, a vertical one for the body, a circle for the head. My eyes drift, trying to find something to latch on to, and alight on the image reflected in the side-view mirror. I try to work out the blind spots Dad's told me about. We have them too.
Blind spots.
Yes, places that gobble everything up, that vacuum us up.

Do you think anyone lives in that farmhouse over there?
Where?
I point to a farm in ruins.
No.
It looks sad. Unless Mom and Ana are there…
Of course they're there. Mom's cooking. You know, making her escalopes in marsala, huh? Yes, she's listening to the radio in the kitchen and her hair is a total mess.
She's wearing an apron.
Did you hear, Mom's calling us. It's readyyyyy! Dinnertiiiiiiime!

Dad and I play a game: inventing our home and decorating it. First of all, it's gonna be big. There'll be loads of windows. And a big yard with a pond full of fish. Me and Ana will have separate bedrooms. Mine will be green and I'll have the space to lay out my collection of rocks. Dad, promise you'll make me a beautiful set of shelves. And I'll put up a big poster of Nadia Comăneci, okay? Okay. There'll be masses of cupboards in the kitchen and Mom can put all her food processors in them. Dad's making shelves for her too. She never has enough room for her recipe books. We'll buy a beautiful gas stove. And there'll be an attic too. Yes. We'll put all the old furniture there. It takes up too much room, don't you think? You're right. And the walls of the living room will be really, really big. Mom will be able to hang all her pictures. I'll make the holes with my drill, I promise. And Ana can finally have the tortoise she's always wanted.

What's Mom's favorite dress? What's Ana's favorite game?
Dad doesn't answer.
The green dress, obviously! And Ana loves playing teachers.

He laughs, he's in a good mood. I take the opportunity to ask why Mom doesn't want to talk to me. He says that when he calls her, she's working, stressed, and they have to be quick because someone's coming into her office.

But if you didn't talk to her for so long, I'd have time for a few words.
Next time, promise.

The trees by the side of the road and in the fields are losing their leaves. The light has been cold for the last few days. We stop in Trieste. Dad's tired. He says he needs a break, to do some thinking.
After driving around for a while, we go to Da Giovanna, a guesthouse near the sea. Dad isn't very patient at the reception desk.
The room with two beds won't be free before two o'clock, the owner says.
Two o'clock? No, that's too long. We've been driving all night... The woman shrugs. Too bad, then. Dad leans down to pick up the suitcase, but Giovanna sighs and gives in, Okay.

The room is large, the ceiling very high, and the walls are covered with pale pink paper... nothing like the dumps over bars. There's even a small armchair and a window that looks out onto the street. Opposite us is a palazzo in white-and-gray stone. For the first time in a long while we have two hot meals a day sitting at a real table in a dining room. It's a room full of books and paintings of boats and rough seas. We're the only guests so we talk very quietly.
It's the low season, Dad whispers.

Giovanna fusses over us. She brings us steaming plates of food and the smell sparks my appetite. *Allora, le mie fettuccine? Come sono? La piccola ha bisogno di mangiare! È troppo magra.* She's saying I'm too thin, and Dad gives a grunt. I stuff my face. You liked that, didn't you? Giovanna eyes him with something like defiance.

That woman's a pain. If she asks you any questions, tell her we're on our way to Lecce and your grandmother's sick. Whatever you do, don't mention Geneva to her, okay?

Dad sleeps a lot. I just draw and when I can't take any more, I wake him.

Our days are spent between the bedroom, the dining room, and walks along the seafront. The sea soothes me, it helps me think. How about you? I'm bored. Come with me! We're going to get a nice pencil case and a beautiful exercise book. At the store I also choose a schoolbag, and I put my new things in it—a drawing book and split-level pencil box with elastic bands to keep the crayons in the right place. Then you can tell at a glance if there's one missing. It's the salesman who recommends it, he's an old man dressed entirely in light gray. He smells nice.

My drawing: a conductor and his musicians. I sketch in their expressions, give the instruments some shape. I hesitate for a moment, draw, erase, start over. My hand searching for something.

Dad wakes me by standing at the foot of my bed and clapping his hands. On your feet! Everybody up, bed made, washed and dressed. Hurry, we're leaving in thirty minutes! Grrr!! He tells me that's how he and his fellow soldiers were woken in the army.
What's going on?

Hurry up, we're going to the station. Did you hear what the bald man said last night? He gave me an idea.

The man yesterday evening?
Yesterday evening I stood by the big window, staring at cars as they slowed at the red light. They were full of condensation because of the heavy rain that had suddenly struck. Everything slithered behind their windshields, the colors, the faces. Impossible to make them out or perhaps only between two vlim-vlams of the windshield wipers, but you had to be quick. People on the sidewalk scurried along, shoulders hunched, heads lowered. Anyone without an umbrella had water dripping down their necks. They turned up their collars, and stepped over large puddles.

Dad was at the bar, immersed in *L'Unità*. "After Reagan Victory, Worldwide Concern." The bar was empty except for a couple at a small table in the corner. The woman had her hair in a bun that reminded me of Mom's. Ana and I called it her "brioche bun." All puffed up and spongy. The woman took the man's hand and gazed at him kindly.

Then a little man burst in noisily. He sat on a barstool and wiped his bald head and the back of his neck with a handkerchief. He spoke loudly. *Un caffè*. He must have been a regular. Do you remember what I told you the other day? he asked the barman. About losing my watch . . . Well, I found it. I remember I took it off on the train. So, on the off chance, I went to Lost Property at the station, and an old guy there handed me a box full of watches. *Figurati* that in among them—there was my watch!
The man held his wrist out across the countertop. See? The barman came closer. It was my father's. It's old, but I can't go anywhere without it. He smiled and kept talking . . . What really surprised me was all the other watches in the box. You should have seen them. Some of them were beautiful! You can say what you like, but there are still some honest people in this country!
Put the coffee on my tab.
The man left in the same way he'd arrived, retracing his steps over his wet footprints.

Dad is pacing up and down. He says, When we get to the Lost Property office, have a really good look at the suitcases, okay? Choose the best one . . . a fancy leather one, and make sure it's big. You have to show you're real pleased to see it again. Go ahead and smile. The man at the office will ask my name . . . which will be . . . Francesco Muravia, okay? Yes, it's a little lie, fine. You get it? . . . If he asks how come I forgot my suitcase, say that . . . that I fell asleep on the train and when I heard them announcing we were leaving the station, I snapped awake and we jumped off the train . . . There, that's how we forgot the suitcase. Okay? We could say it was you who woke me and in the panic we forgot the suitcase. Are you sure you understand?

Back at the hotel, Dad makes a weird face when he opens the suitcase. When he finds jewelry hidden in the lining, he smiles sadly and holds it in the crook of his hand: two bracelets, a string of pearls, and a pair of earrings.

I watch him.
It's a woman's suitcase. Can you smell her perfume? This sweater might suit you, what do you think? He hands me a floaty pink knit.
Ana would definitely like it. But I hate pink.

Dad stops, turns around, bends his knee so he's level with me, and takes hold of my shoulders. I can feel each of his fingers pressing into the tops of my shoulder blades.
My princess, you have to promise me that you'll never tell Mom or anyone else what we're doing here. It's not bad... we're taking things everyone's forgotten about, that's all. It's our secret. Do you promise?

I hate it when Dad tells me stories. To cut him off, I reach for a flat parcel at the bottom of the suitcase and tear open the paper. *In the Fog of Milan,* a book by Bruno Munari. I open it. Several pages of tracing paper overlay each other, creating dense traffic. Everything is gray, then along comes the circus. The pages are brightly colored, littered with holes. I settle into an armchair to read.

Ilaria very disappointed not to talk to you STOP Will call again tomorrow STOP Lunchtime STOP Your husband

---

Trips to the stations are now part of our life, they give us a purpose. The scenario handed to us on a plate by that stranger in Trieste works every time. Dad is enthused, he plays his role. With an authenticity that always surprises, he asks Lost Property offices for watches, bracelets, and necklaces. The staff, drowned by his tide of words, hand over boxes to him. Dad chooses whatever it is he's "lost." *Grazie mille.*

Back in the car, he whistles with satisfaction and pinches my cheek.

It's like you've caught a lost property bug.

Mostly, it's that we need money, princess.

He says it all goes like clockwork because I look so angelic. I'm thrilled he's pleased with me. And anything's better than drifting randomly from one place to the next. Now we're having fun, we have something to do.

Milano Centrale, Bergamo. What about Livorno? And Siena? Did we go there already?

I keep a list of the stations we've visited and another list of the false names Dad has written on the forms. Carlo Micilli. Giulia Grozzi. Marco Bevilacqua. We read the newspaper every day at breakfast. Taking real names as my starting point, I invent new ones, and Dad gives them the thumbs-up or alters them. Once we've agreed, I write them in my notebook, taking special care not to make any spelling mistakes. He hates bad spelling. Last time he really yelled because of a double *p*. I was ashamed.

Now that we stay in three-star hotels I’ve started a collection of mini soaps.

She doesn't have time to talk to you, she hung up. But I was waving at you to pass me the phone, that's not fair. If you didn't talk to her for so long, she'd have time for me too. Next time, I promise.

He's jumpy
He's angry
He's going to get nasty.

In the last few weeks Dad's been getting wound up over the tiniest things. He says he can't stand winter, he can't stand the lack of light. Sometimes he's so angry that I can imagine pétanque balls being thrown around my head. I shudder. And block my ears.
The other day he called me Mom's name, Antonia.

I take my time before I open my mouth now. I start my sentence, watch him, and, if I see the least sign of irritation, I stop.

Answer me when I'm talking to you.
I dither.

I tell Dad that I want to stay here. Okay, but don't move a muscle. I'll come get you as soon as I'm done. In the central concourse of Pisa station, people are clustered under the main departures board. What? What does it say? Where does the train for Milano Centrale leave from? Is my train late? Swaddled in coats and scarves, the crowds are anxious. I sneak into their hubbub, look up and wait for the white letters to appear. Clack, clack, they fall and roll, stop for a moment, form illegible words, then set off again with a whirring sound. What the heck is going on? It doesn't make any sense.

Scusa! A man bundles past me. I turn around. A woman cries, Hurry up! She's dragging a sulking little boy along by the hand. I smile at him and he sticks his tongue out at me. It makes me laugh.
A smell of metal in the air.

Il treno proveniente da Firenze Sant Maria Novella e diretto a Livorno Centrale, delle ore 12.45, è in arrivo al binario 9. Attenzione treno in transito al binario 4.

The black gaps in the departures board remind me of Mauro.
Mauro and his mouth full of black gaps.
We played checkers in a crowded bar near the Livorno harbor. I remember a lovely smell of pasta *al forno* in the air, how much condensation there was, the waitress with her apron tied around her hips serving steaming hot platefuls. She contorted her way between chairs with heavy jackets hanging from their backs. Hot, hot! Then someone yelled, It's time! and all the workmen stood up at once, except Mauro. He stayed sitting. Retired welder and pipe fitter, he said reaching out his big hand before we started to play.

Mauro had a big black gap in his mouth. His front teeth were missing. I lost them because of asbestos. And you need to speak up if you want me to hear you. I also went completely deaf at the factory. So, leaning forward over the table, I asked why he didn't go to the dentist. Mom always says teeth are very important, you have to take care of them. I don't have any money! He laughed and added with a note of pride, Oh, but, you know…I'm not a victim, not me! I'm one hell of a shit-stirrer! He pointed at the walls and some red posters with clear white lettering. Workers' fight. Class war.

When Mauro stood up, he did it slowly, with a groan. I'm rusted all over.

He was tall, his leather jacket very worn, his hands liver-spotted. But what struck me most was the mischief in his eyes. They were the darkest brown eyes surrounded by thick, chaotic eyebrows that curved down so low, right to the corners of his eyes.

I'm a big shit-stirrer!

Mauro. I can still hear his cascading laugh.

As I look at the departures panel, I can't help thinking that it too is rebelling, being disobedient. Disobedient. The word plummets inside me like a stone. It cuts right through me. Something collapses, brings me to life. If I want, *I* could invent words, just like the departures board.

Dad's casualness doesn't have the same effect with gold buyers and pawnbrokers. I don't know why but he goes about it all wrong with them. His voice sounds artificial. But then, these people *are* suspicious, they look just as gloomy as the items displayed in their windows. Hmm, hmm. Can I see? The brisk way they snatch the piece of jewelry cuts short Dad's big speeches. A special magnifying glass brought up to the eye, another brief wait, and the price is slung down onto the counter and left to hover. Take it or leave it. Dad hesitates, protests feebly. Okay. Then it's time for the big lie. He has to claim he's forgotten his ID. You can take me at my word or I'll bring it in tomorrow... It sometimes works. The gold buyers wearily leaf through a wad of money, counting the bills one by one with a smirk. Dad pockets the money and says a frosty goodbye.

Who do they think they are, looking down their noses at me like that? What do they think, I'm some kind of hoodlum? An idiot?

When we hit the road again Dad's in a very bad mood. He always wants me to go with him, but I don't like the way those men look at us.

Are we not going to Rome anymore?
No.
Where then?
To a friend, Giuseppe. It's not far from Rome, in Tuscany. You'll see, he and his wife, Loredana, are very kind, and they have two daughters your age.
But you promised to take me to the Colosseum.
Another time.
You promised to show me the Mouth of Truth.
You promised me a granita on the banks of the Tiber.

Another time, another time, another time.

News for December 19, 1980. The announcer says solemnly: *On the evening of December 18, Rome received the third communication from the Red Brigades since the abduction of Judge Giovanni d'Urso on December 12. As with their two previous messages, the terrorist group denounced the system of special prisons, and particularly Asinara. But the message did not make any specific demands in exchange for d'Urso's release.*

What's Asinara? A prison in Sardinia. "God created hell and, dissatisfied with his work, he created Asinara," that's what people say about it. Terrorists and mafiosos are locked up there. They live in tiny little cells with a bed screwed to the floor and no windows, no table, nothing. But, you know, they're crafty, and they always find some way to talk to each other. Dad laughs and I shudder. Are you cold? Should I put the heater on?

I think about the last Christmas we all spent together.
Mom and Dad fought the whole evening, and Mom decided we needed to get out for some fresh air. We went out in the middle of the night. When we came back, Dad had locked the door from the inside and wouldn't open up.
He yelled at us. Mom, Ana, and I walked for the longest time to find a phone booth. We had to call the police. Mom couldn't stop saying, Why's he making me do this?
Then two big men in dark blue uniforms arrived. They broke down the door and led Dad away, one holding each arm.

Dad struggled, so the policemen used their clubs.
He took quite a beating.
I was out on the landing, I couldn't move. Dad begged me,
Tell them I didn't hurt you. Tell them I'm your daddy!
Then the door to the elevator closed.

The road is full of bends and littered with stones. The headlights bounce in every direction and dust swirls. When Dad cuts the engine, we're outside a long low house that looks like an ocean liner. The air's weirdly warm for December 22, says Dad.

There's a smell of earth, rock, nighttime. I'm anxious. Everything'll be fine, you'll see... their daughters are adorable. The front door opens and the silhouette of a woman with long hair appears, waving us in. Here you are at last! Come in, come in. Giuseeeeeppe, are you coming? Loredana puts her hand on my back and steers me into the kitchen.

Would you like something to drink? Lucia! Maria! Ilaria's here!

Go on, up you go! They're waiting for you.

Standing in the bedroom doorway I first see Lucia's and Maria's faces. They're made up to look like clowns and are buzzing with excitement. Come in! Come in! We're putting on a show for you. They disappear behind a small dormer window, and I look around the room. It's a shambles: toys, plushies, and clothes lying around, socks, crayons, jigsaw-puzzle pieces.

Maria and Lucia keep getting the giggles and have to start their performance again three times before making it through to the end. I clap. We all laugh and then they make up my face, do my hair, and give me a brightly colored costume. You can be... a marchesa!

The Russios' home is so different from the gray of the freeway. The house is surrounded by trees and protected by tall pines. With all those windows it's like living in a light, colorful, transparent bubble.

Loredana and Giuseppe keep saying *amore* to each other. *Amore* this and *amore* that.

In the mornings we're allowed to sleep late and do whatever we want. We have a huge breakfast and then all get comfortable on the living-room sofa to discuss what we'll do in the afternoon. Dad cuddles me close. He seems happy and full of energy. He and Giuseppe spend a lot of time talking in Giuseppe's study. But Dad also joins us for walks and bike rides. He's the one who comes up with the idea of building a tree house. He saws and hammers and hangs curtains. I'm proud of him.

The last rays of sunlight are skimming the outline of the trees in the garden. Shadows are growing longer, and this is the best time for a game of hide-and-seek. Lucia leans her elbow against a tree and counts while Maria slips off to hide behind a tree trunk. I crouch behind the hedges, keeping my head down and my nose between my knees. I don't feel like running, I toy with a twig.

What are Ana and Mom doing this evening? Has Mom bought a big Christmas tree? Has she been shut away in the kitchen for hours making a Mont Blanc for dessert? I clench my fists, I mustn't cry I mustn't cry. I tell myself this over and over and remember what we did this morning. On the way to the beach, Maria told me that Giuseppe invented a tradition for Christmas Eve. We stand facing the sea, hold hands, and make a wish. In silence—that bit's very important. Dad says it'll make next year much better... You wait and see, Dad's always right.

As promised, Loredana comes up to do our hair before dinner. The two sisters have long, curly blond hair that really glows. I sit on the floor with a book in my hand and can't take my eyes off Loredana's hands. Working gently with a stiff brush, she holds the hair firmly to tease out knots at the ends, then uses long brushstrokes to smooth out the whole length of the hair. Like she's caressing it.

Do you still want two braids up in a crown? Lucia nods. Loredana works her fingers deftly. In a few minutes, there are two beautiful braids that start at Lucia's temples, cross over at the back of her neck, and join together on top of her head. It's very very pretty.

Nessun dorma! Nessun dorma! Tu pure, oh Principessa. Nella tua fredda stanza. Guardi le stelle che tremano d'amore. E di Speranza.
Dad sings as he drives, giving his voice a deep resonance. He gesticulates theatrically. He's been in such a good mood since we left the Russios.

We're going to stop. We're almost out of gas. I'll use the opportunity to call Mom. Will you wait for me in the bar?
Okay.

I sit on my barstool and remember our dinner the night before and the pretty drawing book that Giuseppe gave me. On the first page he wrote, "For the best-behaved child in the world" with a little heart and their phone number underneath. The meal was a happy occasion, even if my throat did feel prickly, especially when Dad looked at me sadly and pinched my cheek. He didn't say anything, but we were both thinking the exact same thing, I know we were.

Dad comes to join me. Mom says she doesn't want to talk to me anymore. And if I have anything to say to her, I'll have to go through her lawyer.

She talked like a typewriter. Like I was a stranger.

His hand is all bumpy with swollen veins.

Ilaria wanted to wish you a merry Christmas STOP

In Rome we're staying in a fancy hotel with the front of the building covered in ivy, it's very close to the Piazza Navona. No comparison with small-town hotels. There are bellboys here. When we arrived, one of them took care of parking the car and the other carried our bags upstairs. Our room is number 24, on the third floor. I dance around in circles between our beds, have fun making my toes disappear into the deep-pile carpet, check out the bathroom, sniff the soap, glance at the mirror, and then move in closer. My face has changed. What's different?
Then sobs climb up my throat.
A weight settles in my chest.
Andiamo a fare un giro.

From the city where our daughter was conceived STOP The one you lost in exchange for your freedom STOP And for no other love really STOP You know how I feel STOP Speak soon STOP Your husband

He says the best way to visit Rome is on a Vespa. I can tell he's forcing himself to look happy, putting on this cheerful voice every time we pass a monument. There's "The Typewriter." That's Castel Sant'Angelo. Not forgetting—ta-da!—the Vatican. We hurtle around the Colosseum four or five times, then head to the Piazza del Paradiso for an ice cream. When we return the Vespa, Dad is tired.
Here, he says, handing me some money. Go buy me my newspaper.
I come back to find him lying in the dark.

What are they showing on TV tonight? I open the newspaper, look for something he might find interesting. *C'ere una volta Hollywood* on Rete Uno. They say here it's a montage of all the best bits from musicals. There'll be Fred Astaire, Liza Minnelli, Frank Sinatra, Gene Kelly... and lots more. You'd like that, huh?
Yes. Yes. It could be good.
It's New Year's Day in two days.
Dad turns onto his side and doesn't say another word.

Tre Scalini has become our canteen. When the dessert trolley comes along, Dad lets me choose whatever I want. Chocolate mousse, wild-strawberry tartlets, *crostata di mele*. Then we walk to the museum at the Villa Borghese. Dad wants to see Bernini's sculpture of Apollo and Daphne again and again. He's fascinated by it. He says only a master can carve leaves out of marble and get them right, make them that delicate. He moves closer then backs away. Can you see, Daphne's turning into a tree. If she hadn't tried to escape from Apollo, it wouldn't have happened.

Dad lets me go for walks on my own. One hour, tops.
I always go toward Via dei Coronari. There aren't many cars, I can walk down the middle of the street and pass the store that sells detergent. It smells like home.

Here. Dad just returned from reception. Here, your mother sent you this. I inspect the handwriting on the parcel but don't recognize it. She sent it to your grandmother who sent it here. I tear the cardboard off impatiently. Chocolate eggs fall to the floor. At the bottom of the parcel is a white box containing tubes of paint, a paintbrush, and a block of drawing paper. I recognize the red Caran d'Ache logo.
A shopwindow at Cornavin station in Geneva.
Every time I passed it with Mom and Ana, we stopped to watch the mechanical teddy bears make their jerky movements, holding crayons in their paws. Dad laughs. Well, you sure have enough stuff for drawing. Keep yourself entertained. I'll be back in two hours.
I don't hear him go out, nor the door closing. I let my tears roll down my cheeks. Mom hasn't forgotten me. I smell the parcel. I picture her hands pouring in all those chocolate eggs and decide I should pick them up off the floor. On all fours on that shaggy-haired carpet... and there's a crumpled little ball of white paper under my hand.

"Ilaria. Please call me to tell me where you are. To call me you need to dial all these numbers" (a sequence of numbers).
"I love you and I'm very sad that I haven't seen you in so long. Call me when there's no one around or when Dad's fast asleep. With lots of love from your Mom."

I hesitate. The phone's eyes are staring at me. The hotel's switchboard operator tells me to hold the line. My heart beats very fast. Mom's voice is almost there.
"I'm sorry. There's no reply."

The room becomes a bottomless pit of time. There's no escaping it. Dad has stopped sleeping, he tosses and turns in his bed, switches on the light, talks to himself, yells, insists I not answer. If you say one word just one... he says between gritted teeth. He smokes a lot. The air in our room is unbreathable.
I hug Birillo tightly and pull the sheet up over our heads. Since my attempted call to Mom, since the switchboard operator sold me out, Dad's been drinking a lot and watching me suspiciously. He says I betrayed him, he no longer trusts me. He says, Like mother, like daughter.

To punish me he takes Mom's parcel away one evening and comes back up with a bottle of whiskey. I gave the chocolates and the box of paints to the hotel barman. That'll stop you trying again. He has two children. They'll be happy, you can bet! He stares at me as if challenging me. So, you want to talk to your mother? Is that it?
He picks up the receiver.
Centralino, could you put me through to zero zero forty-one. A bunch of other numbers.

Dad hands me the receiver.

Silence.
Hello?
I hear the distinctive tone of Mom's voice. Everything gets scrambled inside my head. I don't dare utter a single word.

Aren't you saying anything to her?
I make a huge effort, pronounce the word "Mom."
Ilaria! How are you? Where are you? Did you get the parcel I sent you?
Yes. Thank you.
You can do some paintings for me...
Yes.
Where are you?

Dad is leaning over me, he wants to hear every word.
Don't answer that!
I try to move away, but he's holding me firmly by the shoulder.
Are you going to tell her, then?
What?
What you told me.
What?
That you hate her.
Who?
Your mother. Tell her that you hate her.
Dad is scary. I've stopped breathing.

You're going to boarding school next week.
What?
Surely, you don't want to become a brainless idiot?
But—
There are no buts. All children go to school and we're going to buy your uniform tomorrow.

It's January 14, Ana's birthday. Dad's forgotten it. And today's the day he's taking me to boarding school. The sun's beating down.
We wait at the door for a nun to come and open up. The cold freezes my toes trapped in my loafers. You'll see, they'll feel better soon, Dad says, the leather will soften. And stop sniffing. Where's the handkerchief I gave you? My fingers roll around the fabric inside my pocket. Dad pinches my cheek. You'll see, everything's going to be fine. You'll make lots of new friends and don't forget to say thank you and, most of all, work hard.

Dad rings the doorbell several times and I find myself hoping the door never opens.

Dormitory. Six-thirty wake-up. Smooth out the sheet, plump up the pillow, fold down the blanket over the bottom half of the bed. Wash your face, get dressed, walk along the corridor, go downstairs, go into the chapel for Mass at seven-fifteen on the dot. Stifle yawns. Genuflections. Ave Maria. Walk to the refectory without a word. Cookies, tea, clear the table, wipe it. Classes at eight forty-five. Stand up straight, raise your hand. Window, blackboard, window. The sky is full of cauliflower-shaped clouds. Recess. Prayer before lunch. Classes. Corridor, corridor, refectory, corridor, corridor, dormitory. The day ends with a brusque "good night."

My new friend is called Claudia, and we whisper after the nun has turned out the big light. She talks a lot about her older brothers, her bedroom at home, her grandmother, her family. Meanwhile, I can't be sure about the color of Mom's eyes. Blue? Hazel? Claudia has been here for three years. My parents don't want me under their feet, they say with all their traveling they don't have time to take care of me. You too? We're inseparable now. When it rains we stay under the porch watching the raindrops fall into the puddles in the schoolyard. We like the smell of rain but mostly we want to avoid going to the library where Sister Maria sets out crayons for us to color in the Virgin Mary or the baby Jesus. She says it's good for us to learn to stay within the lines. Claudia and I hate it, we hate coloring.

Before I go to sleep I smell Dad's handkerchief and open Mom's note which I hide in a hole that's appeared in Birillo's neck.

While my friends have piano or ballet lessons, Sister Siliana helps me catch up on the schoolwork I've missed. She's all pink and rounded like a peach, with a pointy chin. Her curly gray hair peeps out from her veil, forming a sort of crown. You'll get there, I'll help you, but you need to put your back into this. Concentrate, Ilaria! I repeat after her, calculate, work on my handwriting, do everything I can to please her. You see! That's very good! When Sister Siliana says this, when she puts her plump hand on my shoulder to encourage me, I want to nestle in her arms. I want to tell her I don't deliberately forget things, words fall like snowflakes inside my head and then melt. No, no, I'm not daydreaming. But I can't help myself, I think about that phone call with Mom the whole time. I don't do it on purpose. I wish I could tell Sister Siliana everything. Tell her I'm scared Mom doesn't love me anymore. It wouldn't be surprising, would it? After what I said, she must think I hate her. She can't love me anymore, right?

I'm cold. I need to tell Mom it was Dad who made me say it. This thought opens a window, but it closes again immediately.

If I say anything to Mom, I'll be betraying Dad all over again.

This must be the seventh Saturday in a row that I've waited for Dad in the room reserved for parents. I'm here long enough to watch all the other girls come through, including the older ones I usually see only from behind during Mass. They change out of their uniforms into short skirts, makeup, and colorful scarves.

The nuns try to get hold of Dad. What are they to do with me? Do I have family in Rome? I give them Giuseppe and Loredana's number. Sometimes it takes only half an hour and there he is on his motorbike. Giuseppe smells so good. Sitting on the backseat, I press myself up to his leather jacket and put my arms around his waist. The jolts over Rome's cobblestones make me laugh. I'm scared but I hang tight because I know that I'm about to see Lucia and Maria and I'll forget everything. With them, weekends are like a party. We fill our faces with ice cream, go for bike rides, and put together shows.

When Giuseppe can't come to get me and Dad isn't picking up, the days go on forever at school. While I wait for Claudia to return, I stay in the library and draw or make little books full of scribbles and slip them between the real books. Then life picks up again. Claudia tells me about her weekend at home and, as I listen, I think about the priest who says jealousy is a terrible sin.

Taking a large basin, filling it with warm water, dunking clothes into it and not forgetting to scrub the collars and

cuffs with soap. Rinsing well. Sister Siliana says that otherwise my clothes will go all yellow when they dry.
We climb up to the terrace to hang out our laundry.
The plastic clothes pegs have been eaten away by the sun, some of them snap. Sister Siliana doesn't get angry. She never gets angry.
When we've finished Sister Siliana helps me sit on the low wall. And from up there we can see roof terraces all over Rome. They're full of plants. It's like one big garden.
Sister Siliana points out buildings, domes, bell towers. She knows the names of all the churches.
"Can you see the Colosseum over there?"

For a long, long time I gaze at the open door that leads out to the street, then eventually let the sisters know I'm here. This time, I'm in tears and Sister Siliana takes me to Mother Superior's office. They call Dad together. But it's no good. It's your birthday today, isn't it? We need to do something special! Sister Siliana suggests going to Luna Park. What do you say to that?
Mother Superior doesn't look pleased.
Make sure you're back in time for dinner, *mi raccomando.*
She hands some keys to Sister Siliana.
Yes, Mother.

Sister Siliana grips the steering wheel and knits her brow. I'm not scared, but I have to admit I don't drive very often. True, she's not as assured as Dad. Have you been to Luna Park before? *Mi raccomando,* we mustn't get lost.

There's loud music between the attractions. Bling-blang-blong. Win a scorpion in a bottle! Rifle shooting! Win the jackpot!
Do you want to? Do you want to try? No.
We end up buying caramelized almonds and watching people having fun on the bumper cars. So much happiness is dragging me down, I want to leave. But I don't say anything. Sister Siliana goes to a lot of trouble to make me smile. How about a ride on the roller coaster? Go on! Come! We can't leave without trying one of the rides, can we?

Our red car climbs and climbs and climbs, then glides and drops almost vertically on the rails. The metal screeches and thrums. How on earth don't we go flying through the air? Ooohhh. Ohhh. Ahhh. We laugh and scream very loudly. Again and again and again. It makes me feel fantastic. Another go. Oh, my God! Sister Siliana's voice betrays her fear. I cling to her. She clutches my hand and doesn't let go until we have our feet back on the ground, our heads reeling. A fresh feeling has settled over my chest, I can take big deep breaths. The knot that was crushing me has dissolved.

The sky on this April day is blue. I've already been at boarding school for three months, and Dad isn't here to celebrate my ninth birthday.

Yet another Saturday. The thought of waiting for Dad once again makes me want to run away. What if I call Mom and tell her to come get me? This idea acts like a bucket of cold water poured over my head. It wakes me, fills me with joy. Oh, to leave this boarding school and never come back. To be with Mom again.

I stare at the ceiling and think as fast as I can. Claudia's breathing is regular. She's asleep. I need to go *now*.

I get out of bed, roll up my pillow and slip it under the sheets, then tiptoe downstairs. The door to the patio creeks. Silence. Nothing. The light in the garden is all blue. I run over to the stone wall around the perimeter. If Claudia was with me, we'd be laughing. I regret not saying goodbye to her. My fingers feel for cracks in the stones. Hauling with my arms, pushing with my legs. What about Sister Siliana? What will she think? I jump down into the street. Claudia once told me that when she needs to be brave, she talks to herself out loud. It works every time, I promise. What's that noise? Nothing, keep going, don't turn around. The Colosseum. It's a long way, not all that long, come on, keep going. You'll find a phone booth there and you can call Mom. What's her number? 320 45, no, 342 65. No. I'll remember in the booth. I stop. I forgot Birillo! Mom's number is inside his neck. Keep going. You can't go back there. Head for the next lamppost, don't look at the cars, keep going, don't answer, what are they saying? Mom's voice is over there, at the Colosseum. Just a bit farther, keep going.

The sisters pick me up the following afternoon. The woman who found me told them I'd fallen asleep in a phone booth, in my pajamas.

Sent back.

Tu mi fai girar', tu mi fai girar' come fossi una bambola.
Poi mi butti giù, poi mi butti giù come fossi una bambola.

Dad switches off the radio. Are you coming with me or waiting in the car?
I'm coming. We're in Naples. Dad goes into a tobacconist with a dusty window display full of artificial flowers and brightly colored garlands. Inside, the woman sitting behind the counter has her hair up in a high bun and is reading a photo-story. *Sono Romantica.* How can I help you? Judging by the way she's chewing her gum, with big churns of her jaw, she's annoyed. Her eyelids are purple and her eyes edged with black.
Cesare sent me.
Cesare is a magic word. The woman lights a long menthol cigarette and looks us up and down. She takes her time. Then suddenly blasts her cigarette smoke out through her nostrils like a bull.
Follow me, then. Come around behind the counter.
When Dad reappears he has a sneaky smile. He winks at me, he sold all the jewelry.

We'll sleep here tonight. You lie down on the back seat. He puts his coat over me, sits in the passenger seat, and stretches his legs over the driver's seat. I wake often in the night and have bad dreams. I keep my eyes on the streetlights until I'm exhausted. It's the sun's rays that wake me in the morning. I'm cold, the air is damp, and the windows are covered in water droplets. Dad's asleep. The sticky air makes me want to get out. I walk around the parking lot waiting for him to wake. I find a metal rail and hang upside down on it, wander between the trucks, and then rest my elbows on the fence around the edge of the service station. In the distance farmworkers are digging in a field with mist evaporating from it. The land is smoking. I step over the fence, walk as steadily as I can over and around the clods of earth, shivering, hesitant, and then turn back. My heart's beating very hard.

When I head back to the car, my shoes are muddy, my footsteps heavy.

Dad won't be pleased.

May 5. In transit through the town where you joined me on this day fifteen years ago STOP Still feel the same STOP Infinitely nostalgic STOP Even if spitefulness has gotten the upper hand over our inimitable love STOP
Your husband.

Dad goes around the roundabout once, twice, three times. Then makes up his mind. He justifies why it wasn't left, explains choosing right. He scrutinizes the scenery and the faces of the "morons" who overtake him. He drinks. A swig here, a swig there. He's never without the bottle now, even when he's driving. We're in Calabria, getting close to the Strait of Messina. Just you wait, the road to Palermo's beautiful. It's all along the coast. By lunchtime tomorrow we'll be with your grandmother. Happy?

Up in the mountains the bends make me feel nauseous. I eventually fall asleep.

A few hours later it's dark. I'm lying flat on my front. I'm cold and my head feels heavy. I slowly turn onto my side. From where I am I can see tufts of grass by the roadside and can feel something grainy, tacky under my cheek. The sky's full of stars. I try to sit, give up, then try again. I hurt all over. I bring my hand up near my shoulder, push hard, and my chest finally peels itself from the tarmac. A strangulated voice is calling me. I try to locate it in the darkness, turn my head toward it. Down below me, the car's reduced to a misshapen tin can. It's on its roof. The windshield has shattered. Dad's screaming. Help me, I can't get out. My legs are stuck and the car's leaking gas, I'm scared it'll blow up. You need to hurry.

I try to open the door, but fail. I heave Dad by one arm. He doesn't move at all. Try again. I battle on, hampered by everything I want to say to him, my anger, my need to be with him always, even in a car, even shut up in a hotel room, even with his goddamn bottle of whiskey.

You went through the windshield, the doctor tells me. What's your name? What about my father? Your father's fine. He's with the police. Don't you worry, I'm taking care of you. He disinfects my arms, my leg, my face. And now I'm going to stitch up your ear. You need to be brave, okay? Thread in hand and with a mask over his face, he gently turns my head to one side. I clutch hold of a nurse's fingers, squeezing them as tightly as I can. Seventeen, eighteen... twenty. There we are. All done. Whatever you do, don't move.

It's my thirst that wakes me. I'm in a large room. What happened? Dad's holding my hand. How do you feel, my princess?

I look at him and close my eyes again. A dream sucks me into its world. I'm in a warm room with Mom. We're kneeling at the foot of a Christmas tree, untangling the tinsel. I recognize the furniture from home. I recognize the "boteh" pattern in the carpet, the pictures on the walls. Then another dream begins: Mom is lying comfortably on a lounge chair in a garden. I go over to her, climb onto her lap, and let myself drop against her chest. I'm cocooned by her smell, her arms, the softness of her skin. Mom strokes my hair, brushes my heavy bangs off my forehead. Her fingers are light. The sun warms us both. It sticks us together.

Go spend some time by the sea. You need to rest. Your daughter's still suffering from shock. Before we leave the hospital the doctor gives Dad a piece of paper with the name of a small guesthouse written on it. It's in Scilla. I've called them, they're expecting you.

We arrive by bus, late in the afternoon, suitcase in hand. The car's at a junkyard. I just had time to retrieve a few things. And Birillo. But he needs washing, he smells of gas. And all our cassettes melted.
Dad is very upset.

How long are we staying here? As long as it takes to perk you up. Dad's voice has been flat since the accident. He disinfects my wounds and changes my dressings every morning, and insists I have two good meals a day. I'm not hungry. You need to eat, the doctor said so. If you want to get your strength back, it's the only way.

I have hazy images of the accident, images shot through with bright beams of orange, red, and green. The feeling of danger is still there at night, in the dark. I sleep with Dad, holding his hand. He says yes to everything, even candy.
The little town of Scilla stands on top of a rock that drops vertically down to the sea. On our way to the beach every day we pass a row of white benches with fishermen sitting on them, their faces wrinkled and their eyes full of cataracts. *Buongiorno*. The old men nod. They don't appear to see anything. They sit there waiting, their eyes on the horizon, unblinking, their hands lying over the tops of their canes that are positioned between their legs.

Two weeks go by, two weeks spent watching fishermen caulk their boats and mend their nets, watching the sand drink the sea-foam. I can't swim because of my dressings so I spend hours gathering shells, collecting them in my dress which I hold up over my thighs by the hem. Once this pocket is really full, I drop the whole lot and start a new collection: driftwood, pieces of glass polished by the water.

Dad watches the sea. Sometimes I sit next to him and together we watch the wind whip up the foam, making it twirl in the air. He says I've grown. Says my knees are two balls halfway between my thighs and my calves. Just like a flamingo.

That's what I'll call you from now on. My flamingo.

Dad's trying to be nice. When will he start getting mad again? I'm wary. Sooner or later he'll explode. I know he hasn't forgotten what happened in Rome, what he calls my betrayal. He's unpredictable. The same word can produce two completely opposite reactions in him. Stay on the lookout.

I'm cold.

Come on then, let's go back. It's time to go to the Cosmo.

When we get to the bar I'm allowed a stracciatella ice cream every day, and he's allowed his whiskey. He likes chatting with Gio, the barman. They're both fans of Formula One. They talk about engines, horsepower, tire grip. I read the newspaper while they're talking. Thursday, May 28, 1981. Following the assassination attempt on the pope in the

Piazza San Pietro, the pontiff will remain under strict observation by the doctors at Policlinico in Rome for an indeterminate period. Despite his progress, the pope is showing alarming signs of exhaustion. The date of the next update about his health has not been set.

Dad says we'll be leaving here within the week.

Su di noi, nemmeno nuvola. Su di noi, l'amore è una favola. Su di noi, se tu vuoi volare. Lalala. The singer's right, there isn't a single cloud, but we're not in a fairy story and I *would* like to fly, I really would. It's hot, we're stuck in a taxi and not moving at all. I'm thirsty. The other drivers' faces are dull and tired. Dad's getting riled. Can't you turn the radio down? These ads are unbearable. The driver does as he's asked without a word. His arm is covered in a downy layer of black hair.

Will we be there soon?

We're nearly there. Can you see the palazzo over there? That's your grandmother's house, your first home. That's where you got the scar on your nose.

I run my fingers over the white line left by the injury.

Front door, mirrored doors, wooden doors, glazed doors. Anteroom. Dad stops, presses his ear up to a door covered in fabric. Smiles.

She's watching *Derrick*. Her favorite series.

He looks down, stifles a laugh, pauses. Grandma won't be happy, he whispers. Too bad.

He takes a deep breath, raises his fist, knock knock knock.
Come in.
The room is huge.
Mamma!
Fulvio!
Dad goes over to her. Grandma is lying on a big bed covered in newspapers. Hugging and laughter and so many questions. Photos, plants, clothes on a chair, scarves, colorful necklaces lying on magazines. The mess is indescribable.
Come closer, Ilaria! Come closer so I can have a proper look at you. I take a few steps. Grandma studies me slowly from head to foot and turns to Dad. Your daughter's a carbon copy of you, Fulvio. It's incredible. Dad reaches out his hand to me. Come here, Ilaria, come and kiss your grandma.

Fiery red hair.
The fan goes clickclickclick.
Inspector Derrick says, "Yes, it must be him."

Dad sleeps in Grandpa's old office and I'm in Grandma's. Another shambles, an apricot-colored one. Teetering piles of paper. Pencils and felt-tip pens. Two tables, one of them tilted. Grandma is an architect.
You wait, you'll like it here... you'll find everything you need for drawing. Your father told me you like drawing, right? And look. She opens a large closet full of cardboard

boxes. I've made some room for you here. I read the dates written in felt-tip: 1969, 1970, 1971, 1972. The year I was born. You see! The only thing I ask is that you don't touch my papers, Ilaria, *mi raccomando*.

The apartment is vast. A corridor here, a corridor there, small, medium, and large living rooms for receptions, a dining room, back room, kitchen. This time Dad and I walk down a very narrow corridor and find ourselves in the entrance hall. Its marble floor of black-and-white hexagons is my landmark.

So you see the apartment's split in two. The bedrooms are on one side and all the other rooms on the other. This is the official corridor and that one, on the right, is for the servants. And Vito will come in through there tomorrow, through the service entrance.

Who's Vito?

Um, Vito is Grandma's right-hand man. He does everything. Here and in her office. He's a character! You'll see soon enough, he's quite a talker but he has a heart of gold. He's worked here for . . . forty years?

Grandma is an absolute whirlwind, busy with her work, her bridge games, and her weekends at sea. Wherever she is in the house, I can find her. The clickclick of her heels strikes the ground to the same rhythm as her words, I-have-a-dinner-this-evening-then-a-meeting . . . She's lively, fun, beautiful, in a hurry. She speaks super quickly, rolling her *r*'s and bouncing from one subject to another as she fixes a lock of hair when she passes a mirror. Her fingers are so slender I wonder how her ring finger can cope with the big red plastic ring on it.

Mom would say that Grandma is a hell of a character.
She goes to rest in her bedroom after lunch every day and absolutely no one is allowed to disturb her. Then she returns to work, comes home at the end of the day, gets changed, and heads straight back out. If we see each other, she plants a quick kiss on my forehead and then rubs it with her thumb. Lipstick. She says she'll take me to the hairdresser, she'll buy me clothes, because the ones I'm wearing are too tight all over, and that won't do at all.
I find her intimidating.

"Where aaaaaare you?" "I'm heeeeere!" "I'm off! See you laaaaater." See you later, yes. The front door slams, then the door to Dad's bedroom slams. It's like dominoes falling. A feeling of absence descends.

The best thing is when Vito gets here. The kitchen's transformed into a laboratory with steam in every direction. He has two hours to do the shopping, cobble together some lunch, eat, and put everything away. He's so frenetic that the long strands of hair that straddle his bald patch sometimes tumble down. The first time it happened I had a terrible urge to laugh.

I help Vito set the table and get the trolley ready with plates, bread, salt, water, and wine. He's shown me how to grate the Parmesan on an electric machine. Watch your fingers, *mi raccomando*. Meanwhile, he prepares the vegetables and the meat, cutting things and spinning like a top. He talks a lot, very fast, with this weird way of stopping abruptly. It's like he can see things.

Don't be daunted by Donna L. True, she can be a little domineering, but you know... He casts about for the right words. Either way, one thing's for sure, Donna L. is not a shy, retiring little widow...

Vito tells me it all changed when Grandpa died.

All what?

Everything. Donna L.'s lifestyle, my salary, the schedule. He heaves a sigh. What do you expect? That's life. Things change. He shrugs. Your grandfather was a gentle, refined man. He was very calm. *Un uomo preparato,* an educated man. Another sigh. Poor Signor Fulvio. He's known so much sadness. He stopped halfway through his studies. Everything, he stopped everything. And I don't know whether your grandmother would have coped on her own.

Vito looks up to the heavens and shakes his head. No, without Signor Fulvio, I don't know. Your father's behavior was exemplary. And your grandmother adores him. The minute he leaves she can talk about nothing else. I mean, yes, they have some big fights. But that's just what they're like together. A mother and son . . . you know . . . He gives another shrug.

A long silence.

Vito turns around and tries to look me in the eye.

You know, there's one thing that comforts me. Your grandfather didn't suffer. He went gently with a cup of coffee in his hand, after lunch. Vito picks up a plate and acts it out. Like this, right there in the small sitting room. Donna L. thought he'd fallen asleep, but no, he'd died of a heart attack without a word, sitting holding his cup of coffee. Vito raises his eyebrows, shakes his head from left to right. Donna L. was very strong, she coped with a whole bunch of problems and went out to work with no complaints. For a woman of her standing, that was a big upheaval. Do you understand, Ilaria?

Was Grandpa a lawyer?

Yes, a big one. Shame. Your dad could simply have taken over his practice. With his gift of gab! Oh, he would have been perfect!

Vito takes an old wooden board and a long knife from a drawer.

What are we eating?

Meat and vegetables.

And for dessert?
Fruit. Donna L. doesn't like sugary food. But I bought you some cookies for your afternoon snack. They're in the cupboard.
He fills a saucepan with water, opens and closes the fridge. He's stopped talking now, fully focused on a head of lettuce. He tears it apart, one leaf at a time. I watch his stooped back, the nape of his neck.

Your mother's a brave woman.
How do you mean?
Vito doesn't reply.
Nothing, nothing. Sometimes I talk too much, Ilaria. These are big subjects. Pass me the salad bowl, please. It's there, on the drying rack.
Here you are.
He smiles. Do you know, Illa, a kitchen's really like a confessional. When you lived here, it was Donna Antonia who did the cooking, and she and I talked a lot. She used to make an ex-ceeeep-tion-al chocolate soufflé. You've tried it, right?
Grandma comes through the front door. "Whoooo's at hooooome?" Vito glances at me.
Scram! Donna L. won't be pleased if she knows you're here.

Do it like this, do it like that. Dad shakes his head, pulls a face, glowering at me as he shows me the knife and fork. I copy him discreetly. I wipe my mouth with the big napkin, put my cutlery down at exactly five o'clock on the plate. Mom already taught me all this, but I've forgotten it since I've been with Dad.

The other day Grandma said this to Dad as she got up from the table, Teach your daughter to eat fruit with cutlery. It's intolerable!
I was ashamed. Dad called Vito who came back with a basket of fruit.

It's easy, watch closely how I do it. For example, for a banana, you have to cut lengthways into the peel with the tip of the knife, split it open carefully and then slice the flesh without taking it out of its envelope. Use your fork to eat it. Little slices, see? Then Dad takes a peach, an apple, an apricot. I copy what he does, trying my hardest. He smiles at me. You'll soon be able to eat with the Queen of England.

Special bargain! One kilo of detergent for two thousand lira! I jump out of bed and open the window. It's Tuesday, the soap-seller's day. I recognize his little Ape truck and the electric voice coming from his megaphone. Leaning against the railing, I watch women hand him money. The guy puts white plastic bags onto a large set of scales. And one kilo for the signora. One! *One kilo of detergent for two thousand lira!* I go back to lounge on the mattress. I don't feel like doing anything. Get dressed? What for? To wander around the house? I know it like the back of my hand with its display cabinets of Sicilian ceramics, its engravings, its collection of ladles. Yesterday I opened all the wardrobes, all the drawers, all the cupboards. I even went up to the second floor to see what the little rooms where the servants used to live looked like. Storage space full of dust now, cluttered with cardboard boxes and old leather chests. It was very hot up there and the air was thick with the smell of mothballs.

I looked at some old photos scattered over an armchair. People posing with very solemn faces. The scenery was artificial. Who were they?

Dad, why does Vito eat all on his own in the pantry and not with us?
People don't eat with their servants. I must have looked disappointed.
That's just how it is. It's to do with class. You'll understand when you're older.
I remember what Grandma said when we were eating. A girl should be *graceful*. She should restrain her body. Not make a sound. Sit on the edge of the sofa with her back straight and her legs together and tucked to one side. Wear an appropriate expression.
What does that mean?
Her explanations lost me. She wrapped it all up with, That's how it is. It's a question of upbringing.
There are some things that are "how it is." Like when Dad talks about Mom, Grandma immediately changes the subject.
That's how it is.
That's how it is with boredom too.
I have to find my own solutions. Dad says I'm a big girl, I don't need him anymore. That's how it is. And now that I'm nine and nearly a half, I feel old.

I pass Dad's bedroom and the door is slightly open. I watch him buttoning his shirt very slowly, his face blank. He lives with the window blinds down. The pleasure of being reunited with Grandma is forgotten. He looks limp, sad. He's so thin in his cloud of smoke. Apart from his bed, a coffee table, a chair, a big lamp, and Grandpa's books, there's nothing in the room. Everything in there is earth-toned.

Last week Dad and Grandma talked in whispers for a long time. They didn't want me to hear what they were saying. Dad's shoulders have been heavy ever since. He sighs a lot, more and more. I can see something's not right. He's stopped coming out of his bedroom. If he didn't need to get dressed for lunch, he wouldn't leave the room at all. Mom is an empty bedroom inside his body. On the freeway he used to say he didn't know how to live without her. That she's all he lives for.

He's stopped calling me my princess and my flamingo.

I'm a nuisance to him. Everything's a nuisance to him. His days are at the mercy of the telephone, at the mercy of its dring dring. Dad waits for it, prowls around it like a lion, as if hoping to catch it out, and when it finally rings, he handles the receiver with the tips of his fingers. Like it's burning.

Pronto. His voice is flat. Indifferent. Yes, yes, it's me. Hello, *avvocato*. Granted... Yes... No, she's not going to school. So what?... What difference does it make?... It's the vacation. She's staying here with her grandmother and me. She's very well, yes. We go to the beach every day. Yes... No... I disagree ... Well, then make an appointment with her lawyer ... I'm prepared to go to Geneva if necessary ... No. No. Well ...

Dad's lying, we've never been to the beach.

The air is cool in the small living room. I'm sitting facing the bookshelves with an old sewing box, and I'm stitching together little books using paper Grandma gave me. My head's whirring, I'm enjoying this scribbling, and I'm trying far harder than I did at boarding school. When the pictures look good, I give them titles taken from the books in front of me. I make combinations of words.

No one will ever notice my puttering, but I like walking past the bookshelf and knowing I'm connected to it by a secret.

And there's the old radio set with its big knobs that turn as smoothly as velvet. The little plastic marker shifts along, taking me to Sofia, Tunis, Warsaw. And now I identify a woman speaking English. I think it's the BBC. I understand a word here and there. I've forgotten all my English. And my French too. I speak only Italian now.

Grandma and Dad had a fight this evening before going out to their reception. When she came home from work, she was furious. She laid into him about a ton of different things and shut herself away in her bedroom. He stomped angrily up and down the corridor. He yelled and waved his arms around like the orchestra conductor on TV, with one finger pointing at nothing in particular.

Then Grandma eventually opened her door. Have you finished your little performance? Are you ready? Shall we go? Her voice was clipped, like a slap. Dad stopped dead. Yes.

He stammered. He looked kind of lost. He wished he could say no.

They left arm in arm. Like two actors. Dad in his black tuxedo and bow tie and Grandma with makeup, hair spray, and an emerald green dress with matching shoes.

They left me in the entrance hall.
Ciao, ciao, slam. Bang.
The silence scared me. I closed my eyes for a long time. My body went all stiff. What if I played at sleepwalking? I spun around once, twice, three times and held my arms out in front of me like two planks of wood. Walked forward. My fingers knocked into the walls. I softened them. Small steps. Very small. Glazed door. Cold. Door handle. Cold. I was in the wing with the bedrooms. My feet felt heavy. They were looking for somewhere warm, somewhere comfortable to hide.
Marble, parquet, carpet tufts, smells, sounds.
I walked in a vacuum with a mixture of fear and excitement in my stomach. Hair spray. Sugary perfume. Grandma's bathroom. I fingered her bottles, her tubes of cream, prickled myself on the bristles of a brush. The carpet under my feet was soft and warm, then it became scratchy. It was such a strange feeling in the middle of that sea of softness that I cheated and opened my eyes. Yes, my big toe had been right, there definitely was a patch the size of a round loaf of bread, it was all worn and showed glimpses of the gray

weave. I looked up. Six mirrors. Big ones, little ones. They knocked the breath out of me. And now I understood how Grandma always looks perfect. Standing here, she could see herself from the front, from the back, and in profile. My six bodies didn't want to leave. Were they really mine? I closed my eyes very tight, felt my way to the bath, and slid into it. But that too felt horrible. Quick quick get out of there. Door, corridor, door. Smell of cold tobacco, and anger, and waiting. That was Dad's room. No, no, no. I found the marble of the entrance hall again. The lines between the black-and-white squares led me to the plants. I stroked their leaves and stems. They were warm. There was a nice smell of damp soil. I crouched down between two pots.

Dad and Grandma fight all the time. Their subjects: the astronomical bill at the Hotel de Rome that Dad never paid, the accumulated bills for the telephone and whiskey. And why don't you look for a job? Why don't you go out with Ilaria? What are you planning to do with the child? She could have tennis lessons…And what about school?
I've become a soccer ball between them.

When Dad answers Grandma's questions, the walls and floors shudder. She takes refuge in her bedroom, turns the key in the lock, and Dad goes crazy.
He becomes this screaming voice.
He sweats, splutters, gesticulates, yells.

I don't want to see the muscles in Dad's jaw tighten. I don't want to hear his teeth grind. I don't want to keep holding my breath, feeling his yells batter my temples. And a knot in my throat.

Illa! Illa! What are you doing there? That's very dangerous! Come on, come back inside.

Old Vito, dear old Vito, Vito's voice.

My knees are shaking. When I climbed out across the roof I wasn't scared, but now that I have to retrace my steps I'm paralyzed. My head's spinning. Vito guides me. Don't stand up. Lean on your hands. Stay sitting. Just raise your backside, only as much as you need to, no more. Slowly, slowly I reach the skylight. Vito takes me in his arms. And I cry, even though I swore I'd never cry again.

Promise you won't say anything to Dad?

Vito promises. He takes my hand and we go downstairs, Vito in front, me behind. Would you like me to make you something to eat? Sit yourself down and tell me what you were up to on the roof. He rummages in the cupboard, takes out a packet of cookies, and puts them on a plate. Here you are. He puts a pan over the burner and fills it with milk. Shall I make you a fruit salad as well? He smiles. Strokes my cheek. Well, help me then. With the basket of fruit in front of us, we peel and chop apples, a banana, and an orange. Then Vito halves a lemon, drives a fork into the flesh and squeezes out the juice.

Eat, my child.

Grandma's back slouches as she sits on the edge of the bed. Her face is turned toward the window and her elbows are resting on her knees. She's looking at the floor. She didn't hear me come in. Oh, it's you. Come here, come sit next to me. She pats the bedspread. Her face looks almost anguished. I've just been talking to Isabella. She's a very old friend. You have your own best friend, don't you? She doesn't wait for me to answer. Isabella's agreed to look after you. She lives in the country, two hours from here. I'll take you there. She's on her own and you'll keep her company.

She stands up, walks past the mirror, straightens her hair, making a funny pout with her mouth, like a chicken, and says, Dad has found a job. That's a lie, I know it is. You can't stay here, alone all day long. Come on! I'm going to get ready. I follow her into the bathroom. Looking into the mirror on her dressing table, she takes a ball of cotton wool, powders her face, brushes her hair, sprays it.
We're going to do some shopping. You can't go to Isabella dressed like that. Go get changed, we're leaving in five minutes.

In the elevator she takes me by the chin.
I really like you, my little Ilaria.

Mi raccomando, be very polite and do as Isabella says.
Mi raccomando, make your bed every morning.
Mi raccomando, mind your table manners, brush your hair, and clean your teeth.

In the car Grandma hammers her recommendations into my head like nails. I'm thinking about Dad, and how we said our goodbyes. You're lucky to be going to Isabella. She's a great lady, you know.
He promised he'll come visit me. And call me too.
Don't sulk, Grandma says as she turns on the radio.

The announcer: *Today, September 9, 1981, Picasso's famous painting* Guernica *has returned to Madrid after spending forty years at the Museum of Modern Art in New York.*
Grandma explains that it's one of the most important paintings in the world. Huge, huge, huge. Remember that name, Ilaria. Pi-ca-sssso.

Two hours and then three. After the main roads, we get lost on country lanes. I don't know how Grandma finds her way in this place full of hills, white rocks, and yellow grass. Everything is dry and there are no signs to give us directions. Ah! I think we're getting close now. It's over there, can you see? She points at a patch of green. You know, Ilaria, I think spending some time in the country will do you nothing but good. Just think, you've spent the whole summer shut up indoors. That's no life for a child, is it? She turns to me with a chuckle. Her red hair is a complete mess. It looks like a housefire. Yes, I'm sure you're right. But, you see, I don't know Isabella. Don't worry about that. You'll soon see, she's adorable.

Her car, an old banger, is shaking all over. The metal creaks. The cushion on the rear seat falls off.

Leave it... it's my tenant's cushion.

Your tenant? What's a tenant?

It's a man who sleeps in my car every night. We reached an agreement: So long as the car is kept clean, I let him sleep in it. He can't sleep on the sidewalk, can he? she says, laughing. Grandma is beautiful, and impatient.

I hate coming here. I always get lost. Make sure you do a nice curtsey for Isabella, *mi raccomando*.

We arrive at last. Long driveway, stone arch. I read the name of the house engraved in a square of white marble. La Ninfa. The Nymph.

Grandma parks in the middle of the courtyard and the great lady comes to greet us. Isabella is wearing a beautiful, loose white dress and sandals. Smiles, bowing, approval in Grandma's eyes, a kiss on each cheek and there she is back at the wheel of her old banger.
Vroom-vroom, Grandma's off, waving her hand out the car window. A glint of light on her big red ring.
Ciao ciao!

Isabella and I stay rooted to the spot, watching the cloud of dust in the drive settle. I feel like an idiot. A bulky parcel, in the way. Should I say something? Isabella raises her shoulders. Bah! Your grandmother's quite a character.
Dad had said, "Isabella's a great lady." What with the *great lady* and the *real person,* will I get this right?

Then Isabella points at the sky. It's like her head's being pulled backward by invisible string. Do you hear that, Ilaria? I strain my ears. Yes, piano playing. It sounds like waves, don't you think? I love this passage. Come on, let's go in! She takes my suitcase and we climb the steps to the front door.

The house is enormous, a new labyrinth of small and large sitting rooms and high ceilings decorated with false skies and pink angels. Corridors, rooms. Everything is white and, as Grandma had said, sparsely furnished.
The piano in the distance accompanies us.
It'll take you a few days to get your bearings, that's to be expected. The house is horseshoe-shaped but we only use one wing, do you see? Isabella points through the window to the closed shutters opposite. It would take a lot of work to get this building back on its feet and get rid of the damp. Too bad.

When we reach the doorway to my bedroom, Isabella introduces me to Paola, the housekeeper.
Paola, may I introduce Ilaria.
I make a curtsey.
Paola will come get you in fifteen minutes for dinner.

Nightstand. Smell of lavender. Desk. Chair. Large window looking out over the courtyard. A tabby cat walks across it.

The wool blanket on the bed prickles the backs of my thighs.
Silence.

From that first evening, I make sure I sit up straight and use the correct fork. My head is full of all Grandma's advice and Dad's sideways glances. It's quite a commotion in there. Isabella tells me that she goes into the village every day. It's twenty minutes away and I'd be welcome to join her if I like. And I'll expect you here for meals. Eight in the morning for breakfast, one in the afternoon for lunch, and eight in the evening for dinner.
There's talcum powder in her voice. Like Chet Baker. Loneliness, Dad would say.
While she talks, my eyes are drawn to the portraits all around us. The faces are pale and rounded, the chests laden with gold embroidery. They're her ancestors. That's my mother, that's my father, my grandfather, and my aunt, over there is my great-uncle. He was a pope. Isabella laughs. They look strict, don't they? But they're all dead and buried. Isabella flushes and puts a hand to her mouth, as if she'd said something terrible.

If you want to read, there are lots of books in the library.
I have my drawing book.
Isabella smiles.
Will you show me sometime?

The wool blanket scratches my legs, even through the sheet. My bed creaks and there's a spider in a corner of the ceiling, right above my head. When Paola comes to say good night, I point it out to her anxiously. She laughs. It won't hurt you. I can't help imagining that in the dark the spider will drop down to my level and sidle between the sheets. It will bite me and I'll be covered in big blue blotches.

I hug Birillo to my stomach. Just stop thinking about the horrible critter.

The night outside creeps into the room. Grasshoppers. Unless maybe they're crickets. An owl hooting.

I go to sleep with the light on.

Isabella goes to the village every morning. This very distinguished, elegant woman sure looks strange in her green jeep. She comes back with packages in her arms, sometimes vegetables, bread, the newspaper. Paola says that Isabella goes to see the priest. That her husband's death caused her a lot of pain. That she's unrecognizable and the house has never been so empty. She also says, Before I used to spend my whole time making and unmaking beds, washing sheets, and preparing meals for guests. La Principessa entertained a lot. Now she doesn't go out much and just listens to sad music in the pink sitting room. Isabella must have called it that because of a woman's dress in the large tapestry. The embroidered woman is seen from behind. She's wearing a triangular hat and standing by a well. A smiling young man faces her, holding a bucket. Behind them, forest, branches, leaves, stones, patches of sky.

I sit in an armchair with a book on my lap, unable to read. Isabella is knitting. She reminds me of a valuable glass—long, slender, upright, cold. The streak of white that starts at her forehead gets lost in the salt-and-pepper of her hair. When we make eye contact, I smile, and so does she. She must be shy. Her eyes are gentle, turquoise, piercing.

Can you knit?

I shake my head.

Would you like to learn?

No thank you. But I'm intrigued and join her on the large sofa.
Look, one stitch to the front, one to the back.
Her fingers are agile, swift.

Coming out of the forest, we've found a beautiful fig tree. And Birillo has called it Camillo. We had to walk through the pines for a long time and follow a dusty path beside a grove of olive trees with gnarled trunks. Then we stepped over a low wall smothered in brambles.

And now here's Camillo, huge, a ball of fleshy leaves. Its branches skim the ground and the big stones there, but they also reach high into the sky.

No one will come looking for us here. We can holler as much as we like . . . there's nothing here but birds, ants, and green lizards that run between the stones, freeze, then continue on their way. Birillo doesn't like them, but I reassure him. Nothing can happen to us when we're ensconced at the top of Camillo. I take off my socks and watch them fall.

Birillo, if no one can see us do we really exist?

Birillo doesn't answer.

What's Dad doing now? I miss him. No, no . . . that's not true. I can hear his rifle-shot mouth. Taratatarrra. His grinding teeth. His hurtful words.

Birillo tells me not to think about anything. Don't think about Mom either, or Ana.

They're getting hazier and hazier. I can't picture their faces. Birillo says what matters most is that we're together.

I'll never leave, he whispers. I hug him and slip one of Camillo's leaves into the hole that appeared at the base of his neck when we were in boarding school. I've never stitched it up because it's a perfect hiding place for my mementos. Little messages, Mom's note, leaves. What else?

Come on, let's go.
Back we go with sandals covered in dust and sticky hands.
And wonderful figs in my pockets for dessert.

Isabella's worried I'll ruin my clothes. She asked Paola to take me to Ninì, the peasant woman who lives with her husband, Corrado, in the house next to the barn. They work la Principessa's land and tend the vines. You wait, Ninì has hands of gold, she'll make you some pretty skirts.

Gripping the tape measure between her teeth, Ninì took my measurements and noted everything down on a piece of paper. Before I left, she asked me to help her put some big planks of wood onto the table outside and one thing led to another, so I stayed to help her spread out the tomato puree. We used our fingers to smooth out the lumps and ease a thin layer of puree over the wood. Then we sprinkled this sea of red with salt and covered it all with a piece of very fine fabric. We'll leave it to dry for three or four days, it's for tomato concentrate, Ninì explained.
At the end of the morning, my palms were all wrinkled.

Since then, I've gone over every morning to see if Ninì needs help. Corrado leaves at dawn. It's nearly time for the grape harvest. There's a lot to do.

Every last cloud has been swallowed by the blue of the sky. The color is so dense that nothing else exists overhead. Ninì wipes her forehead in the crook of her elbow.
Would you like to feed the hens? I can hang out the sheets while you do that. She goes to fetch a bucket.
You have to crumble it in your fingers like this... Watch how I do it.
Pioooo, piooooo! Choocks...
The hens come running, clucking. You try. She hands me the bucket.
What is it?
Wet bread.
I hesitate, then delve into the claggy slop.

Isabella has decided that I really should know how to count, and I now have to recite my times table to her *every* morning.

3 × 7 =
5 × 20 =
4 × 9 =

I'm so scared of getting it wrong that everything becomes jumbled in my head. I can hear Sister Siliana saying "Concentrate" like she did at boarding school, but I just can't. The numbers unravel, turn into curves and straight lines. Everything sticks together and the result is illegible. Isabella eventually lost her patience and one morning she handed me an exercise book.

Try to write, maybe you'll find it easier. On paper, the numbers have a beginning and an end. She's right, it all calms down. Using my hands, I can see and think better.

Isabella encourages me. Two more questions and I'll let you go.

4 x 9 = ?
8 x 6 = ?

Isabella knows I like going to see Ninì. I enjoy being immersed in her world, using my nose, my ears, and my fingers to help her make preserves, work the soil in the vegetable plot, or turn over the hay in Turri's stall, he's Corrado's mule. As well as all this, Ninì transports me to a different world with her stories about witches. She tells me they really exist and the forest is full of them. When I told her I sometimes walk there, she ran to me and threw salt over my left shoulder. The next day a little pouch of fabric was waiting for me on the kitchen table. It's filled with two teaspoons of flour. You should wear that around your neck to scare them, otherwise the witches could really hurt you... Ninì says I'm *una piccirridda,* a city kid, and I know nothing about the spirit world. Whether or not that's true, what I care about is seeing her tilt her chin and knit her brows, and listening to her explain how to hold a pitchfork, dig up potatoes, and cut onions. Try, she always says "try." With her I'm not scared of saying the wrong thing, we laugh together. Her eyes are playful, mischievous. And she can do anything with her hands. She can sew, make orange marmalade cookies, and work out how much time is left till sunset. She just puts her fingers between the bottom of the sun and the horizon, squeezing them all together... and there's the answer, Another thirty minutes.

Ninì's hands know a ton of things.

Mangia, Ilaria. Brava, Ilaria. And then after thirty minutes Corrado appears on the dirt path with Turri. They draw closer without a sound, their backs to the sun.

Bonasira! Corrado jumps from his cart outside the house, takes off his cap, and runs his hand through his hair which is plastered to his head by the heat.

Then he unhitches Turri and strokes her. She stretches her neck, shakes her head, scattering flies, and makes a sort of whinnying sound. Do you want to take her? Go on, go with Ilaria. He hands me the reins. Come on, Turri, come along! I've made your bed of straw and changed your water. I talk to her gently, like Corrado. You can rest now.

Corrado does the same repetitive things day after day. He doesn't talk much. The goats are fine. The grapes are nearly ripe.

Taking a bath, brushing my hair, dressing for dinner. And quickly, water is precious. As soon as I'm in the bathtub Paola comes to wash my back and behind my ears. You can get ticks there, Ilaria. The hip bath has a rough surface. Her movements may be brusque and she always has this disgruntled look on her face, but Paola is affectionate in her own way. Dad would say she has a thankless face. But I can see kindness in her gray eyes and those cheeks covered in little red veins. It's true, she does mutter and she has a funny way of slicing bread, holding it right up to her chest. So what?

Paola doesn't have children and Ninì gently makes fun of her. Well, you married la Principessa, so what do you expect? They chat about sewing and family. That's how I know that Ninì's children are grown up and live in Palermo. She has a girl and a boy.

When Paola comes to Ninì's house with me, she always produces something from her apron pocket, something she's sewn, knitted, or cooked. And as I watch her, I think that what she's giving Ninì is her free time. Ninì thanks her, and Paola screws up her face to mean she's welcome.

Today it's some red flowers embroidered onto a square of white cotton. So that the grape harvest begins well.

We've washed the baskets and the knives used for cutting bunches of grapes, and we've heated water in big pans to sterilize the barrels in which the grapes will be crushed underfoot. The children get that job, you can help us if you like, Ilaria. Everyone gets involved with the grape harvest! Farmers, stockmen, neighbors, friends. Ninì's so happy.
And then when it's all done . . . there's a party. You wait. Even la Principessa comes.

It's six a.m. The yard is a hive of activity, but it's still steeped in morning silence. The men are tending to the mules, the women loading piles of wicker baskets onto the carts, and children my age are filling small boxes with snacks that the men take to the vineyard with them. The youngest kids are wrapped up in shawls, playing happily on a bench.
We're waiting for Corrado's signal to set off.
Amunì! Amunì! Off we go. His voice thunders.
Amunì! Amunì! Let the harvest begin. The men sit on the backs of the carts with their legs dangling. They're smiling.

I stroke Turri one last time. Safe travels, Corrado.
His eyes crease. Behind his lips he has beautiful white teeth. He's happy.
Are the vineyards far away?
Forty minutes from here. Would you like to come?
No . . . no . . . I'll stay here.
Tomorrow?
Maybe.

Children jog along the road, some of them are going with the men.

The first full baskets arrive at midday. The sun is biting. Men stand in the carts carefully emptying the grapes into other baskets. The women work in pairs to carry these into the barn.
The bunches of grapes don't make a sound as they fall.

It's now our turn, the children's, to do our work. Two by two we heave ourselves up into our barrels. I'm with Chiara, a chubby little blond girl. *Guarda, accussì, accussì*. Look, like this. She lifts her legs very high and holds her black skirt to her hips to avoid staining it.
We're wearing nearly the same outfit. Ninì made it for me, including the pretty white blouse with bell-shaped sleeves that puff at the shoulders. She gave it to me yesterday evening.
I gave her a big kiss in the crook of her neck before racing off to try it on, and she hugged me. Her body was warm. A gift.

The grapes burst under my feet, get wedged between my toes. They're soft and it tickles. There are peals of laughter in every direction. The women are busy all around the barrels, changing the bowls that the juice pours into. Jump, children, jump! They talk loudly, help one another, and call to one another. The barn's swarming with activity.

Out of nowhere a young woman starts singing. Her black silhouette in the doorway stands out against the sun flooding in behind her. Her voice is deep, sweet, and powerful. It's so beautiful that everyone stops, holds their breath.

Seven days of waking at dawn, seven days of laughter, work, and cooperation. Going through the same motions, more numbed by exhaustion every day.

Then the party.

Isabella is here too, sitting *a capo tavola,* at the head of the table. She listens, answers, asks questions. She smiles the whole time and drinks several glasses of wine. The tables are covered with fruit and empty plates. No one has the strength left to clear them. Who cares? The musicians are taking their positions, the dancing's about to begin.

Intimidated but helped by the wine, Corrado asks la Principessa to dance. *Una tarantella?* Isabella holds out her hand and stands up, he bows to her and takes her by the waist. Other couples get to their feet. Corrado and Isabella have opened the ball.

Lu vino fa cantari, l'acqua fa allintari.

Wine makes you sing, water makes you falter.

Paola has rolled the carpet back out after beating it in the courtyard. I helped her. Winter's on the way, look at the sky. Can you see? The light's different, the sun's lost its edge. Night falls faster. There aren't so many butterflies.
The leaves on the creeper that covered the whole house when I arrived have fallen. All that's left are the bare branches, the plant's nervous system, which traces curves and triangles.

Her hands move lightly when she picks up her porcelain cup and saucer. She holds it close to the sugar bowl, drops in a good spoonful of sugar, stirs the cup without a sound and puts a thin slice of lemon into it.

Now that the sun's setting earlier, we've gotten into the habit of watching an episode of *Pippi Longstocking* at tea-time, and only if the temperamental antenna will let us.

Isabella has just as much fun as I do watching Pippi's fooling around, even though it can be a little ridiculous. She curls up in a ball on the sofa and hides her smiles behind her hands. I actually think she sometimes flushes with pleasure. She looks like a child eating a big cotton candy. I'm pretty sure she always sits up so straight because of her ancestors, but when she's watching Pippi she forgets about them.

When Isabella reads out loud, she straightens her back, clears her throat, and takes deep breaths. With the book resting on her knee, she turns a page, two pages, three, and glances at me to check I'm there, with her. Then she reads on, with a smile in her eyes.

When Isabella reads, all of her flows with her breathing, slowing and accelerating. Every word lands inside my body, opening it, sending it to sleep. Images spool past behind my closed eyelids. I become the sea, I become a thread, I become a whale, I become salt.
When Isabella reads, she moves her shoulders and her hands. She pauses, follows the sentences with her body, undulates. Do you like it? The sitting room fills with air, the wind whistles oooooohooo oooooohooo. Isabella pretends to stop and looks at me. I frown. Please go on. I'm just about to jump in and swim. Don't stop.

The library, which previously gave me the shivers, now entices me. If every book contains its own world, how can I do this? Will I have time to read them all? Where can I put all these new sensations?

When I'm tucked up in bed after our evening meal, the story comes back to me. I try to arrange the images and, some evenings, a completely different story takes shape. I add in characters, details, and words. It's like Nadia Comăneci's routines. To expand the tale, you have to push the boundaries, disobey logic, find the point where the body tips and achieves a new kind of balance.

Dad called. Just hearing his voice, I could picture him in his room with his elbows on his knees, surrounded by a cloud of smoke.

He said he's coming to get me tomorrow.

Packing my bags. Paola has taken charge of things. Ninì is sitting on a chair and has nestled Birillo in the folds of her apron.
She doesn't say a word and I'd rather not look at her.

After the goodbyes and once Dad has set off down the drive, I turn around. Paola, Isabella, and Ninì are standing, framed by the rear windshield. They form a pyramid. Isabella is in the middle and on either side, her two pillars. The farther we go, the smaller they become.

They are a rock. My invisible rock.

Christmas. The table gleams all over. We're expecting guests.
Vito's making the meal. He's wearing his white jacket.
There's a smell of wood fire.
It's the only evening of the year when the fire's lit in the hearth, Grandma says with a chuckle.
Nothing here has changed. Except that Dad's working.

What's stopping me from hating Dad? The shame I saw in his eyes the day I was so infuriated by his whiskeys that I emptied his bottle of Ballantine's down the basin in the bathroom. And I replaced the yellowish liquor with water.

After drinking a long slug straight from the bottle, Dad looked at me out of the corner of his eye. Then looked away, without a word.

I've been back at school for a month.
Sitting still is pure torture. I think about the countryside, the birds, the sirocco, the dust on the dirt roads, the huge sky overhead. About Ninì. Isabella. Paola. And I make drawings of Turri in the margins of my exercise book.

The nun shows us Syria on the geography map. She asks us to stand and pray for this faraway country and the inhabitants of Hama. She says they're being massacred by their president, Hafez al-Assad.

Dad forgets to come pick me up at school. I wait thousands of minutes for him every day. When he does arrive, he says, Stop being so melodramatic, stop your tantrums. I couldn't get here sooner, I have my work, you know. I remember those Saturday mornings at boarding school. But this time around, the inner courtyard where I wait for him is a black hole that sucks me in. It expands, I fall, my breath becomes erratic. What would Pippi do?

Now that Dad's found work, he drinks too much and yells all the time. When he's home, he says his boss is an idiot, and he has to put up with him, it's humiliating and no one has faith in him. He buries me under his terrible mood and gives me orders.
Take my glasses back to the kitchen.
Go fetch me a bottle of water.

He's mean.
Yesterday I said no, once, twice, three times.
With a sarcastic half smile, Dad let me put up my resistance, then his face contracted. He spat at my feet. His eyes were two metal lances.
Who do you think you are?

I write:
Not setting foot in school again. Never talking again.
Never eating again.
And I slip the piece of paper into Birillo's neck.

My head hurts. My stomach hurts. I refuse to eat.

I've learned to be absent, to withdraw from my hand, my arm, and my toes, to send every muscle in my face to sleep, embed my legs into my body, become a trunk, bury myself in the dark. Since learning to do this, I feel safe. I just have to close my eyes, concentrate a little, and my nerves become numb, they switch off. I stop feeling anything. No sights, no sounds. My body's behind a window, unreachable. The world can keep on turning, I've stopped existing. I've canceled myself.

Ilaria, Ilaria, what are you doing? Dad's worried. For the last two weeks, I've stayed lying down, my face turned to the wall. Vito comes to see me. Illa, Illa, talk to me. I don't reply. He makes chicken stock for me and I can barely swallow it. Call the doctor, Grandma orders. The family doctor examines me, turns me every which way. Apart from the fact that I'm thin, everything's fine. His conclusion: He pokes his temple with one finger. It's all going on in here.

He comes up with everything and anything to get me out of bed. Let's go buy an ice cream. A jigsaw puzzle? New pens! Let's go out for some cigarettes. We'll take the car. Come on. I need some batteries too.
That day I say yes. For no particular reason.

Outside the tobacconist's, a police officer comes over to us.
Are you Fulvio and Ilaria L.?
Yes. Dad's voice is expressionless.

Come with us.
We get into separate cars.
In the car, I think to myself they must have found out we stole watches from train stations. How many stations were there? When the car stops, I've counted fifteen.

At the precinct, a female officer points to a chair for me. The questioning starts.
What have you been doing these last two years?
Where were you?
Who did you live with?
And where did you go after Rome?
Why didn't you contact your mother?
Really? Didn't you know she was looking for you?

I hate this woman.

She says that, while we're waiting for Mom to get here, they're going to put me in an institution. What's an institu-

tion? An orphanage. You need to be protected from your father. The phone rings. Okay, okay.
You're going to stay with a friend of your mother's until she gets here. That's settled.
She'll be here the day after tomorrow.

Sitting looking at the piano, in a living room.
Mom comes in.
I stand up, I walk toward her, I move faster.
My heart beats as fast as it can. We look at each other.
Something's changed. You've grown so much. Those are her first words. I recognize the sound of her voice. In her arms I'm reunited with her smell. Then Dad shows up, and Grandma and Vito. There's also a man, a lawyer. Dad and Mom hardly even say hello to each other.
Vito hands me Birillo and smiles.
Dad and Mom are facing each other. They don't take their eyes off each other. Mom crosses her arms over her chest. I look at the carpet, counting the shapes. Three blue lozenges, two red lozenges, three blue lozenges, two red lozenges, three blue lozenges, two red lozenges. My stomach is swollen, hard. I think about the eyes of that doll we bought for Ana in Turin. I think about her long plastic eyelashes that snapped shut, just like that. Clack. Then the lawyer clears his throat. Ilaria. Ilaria. I don't look up. He talks and his voice is an electric shock that goes on for hours. I hug Birillo close. The lawyer puts his hand on my shoulder. He's asking me something. He repeats the question, kneels down, tilts my chin up with his finger. His eyes bore into mine. Who do you want to go with. Mommy or Daddy?

I look at the tips of Dad's shoes, then Mom's.

I retract, retreat to my cave. Head deep into the darkness.

Give her some time to think, says Dad. He goes over to Grandma. No one in the room breathes. The air is full of concrete. Dad walks away. There's a clinking of glasses. Liquid flowing. Then I see Vito's shoes go over to him. He whispers something. I don't hear what he says. Dad doesn't answer, then crouches down to my level. I can feel his heavy breath.

Go with Mom. You'll be better off with her.

When he hugs me, I catch his smell of alcohol. And sweat. And tobacco. I catch the smell of his fear. His tears.

His hands are clammy.

In the plane everything's dark. I curl up on my seat and lie across it. Rest your head here. I rest it on Mom's lap. She strokes my hair and kisses my forehead. Says she's happy she found me. Says she looked for me so hard, she's relieved.

I change my position, rest my head against the window. My back hurts. I can't work out how to sit.
What's Dad doing? And Vito? And Grandma? And Isabella? And Ninì?
Mom hesitates, then takes my hand.
If you want to go back to see your father, I'll take you, I promise.

The parking lot at Milan airport is enormous. It's night-time and it's cold. Mom looks lost. I don't remember where I parked the car. What color is it? Gray, the car's gray. While we walk, she explains there were no direct flights from Geneva to Palermo so she drove here. But I can't remember anything. Mom's tired. Her voice is flat.

We reach Geneva at daybreak.

I'm hanging upside down from the rail. The bell rings. My palms are on the asphalt when I see a pair of shoes coming over. I don't recognize them but I do recognize the voice. It's Ana.

Mom orders steak and, for dessert, meringues with whipped cream. I'm not hungry. We talk in Italian, then Mom and Ana forget and go back to French. I listen, struggling to understand. The words are slippery, they fall under the table and push me behind a thick pane of glass. Nothing's like I remember. Their faces are new, but also familiar, all muddled up.
Ana's wearing a red T-shirt and her hair's grown. She has a ring with a small green stone on her finger. She's grown. Mom's face looks drawn. The last two years have carved dark bags under her eyes.
She's different too. In what way? I don't know.

I clutch Birillo.

We don't talk about what happened. No one asks me anything and I don't ask anything either. The word "Dad" lingers under our feet. A piece of glass. To be avoided. The day after tomorrow there's school. We need to think about a schoolbag, and shoes, buying me a jacket. Mom has taken time off work to do some shopping.

Ana's laughing, but my mind's drifted, I missed her joke. I need to get used to them now. Dad will morph into a room inside me. I'll keep my memories there. Or maybe he'll become just a dot. Or masses of dots like the wallpaper in my bedroom.

Someone in the restaurant turns up the volume on the radio. Franco Battiato. "Cerco un centro di gravità permanente."

TRANSLATOR'S AFTERWORD

Over my years as a translator, I've developed a habit of writing an appreciative note about the book to my editor when I deliver the finished translation. It will describe an aspect of the book that I've particularly enjoyed—the voice, the narrative arc, the scene-setting—and it may well diplomatically sidestep aspects of the translation that have been gruelling or in some cases, let's be brutally honest, tiresome. Then, even with books I've really cherished, I don't tend to look forward to being sent the edits. It's not that the process is irksome: it's usually straightforward and gives the text added value. It's more because I feel I've had closure with the characters and there's something indecent about raking over syntactical quibbles rather than fully engaging with them again.

I was so taken with the character of Ilaria, though, that my note to the editor read simply, "No need for a long spiel here: I have JUST LOVED translating this little book and I look forward to being reunited with Ilaria for the edits and the proofs!" How could I fail to re-engage with this child even if only scanning past her to correct a typo or tighten the syntax of a sentence?

Ilaria is one of the most endearing and credible children I've met in literature, and in translating the text I was keen to honour this unforgettable character and her engaging narrative voice. This pragmatic, vulnerable and often bewildered child is pushed from pillar to post in an adult world, making sense of it as best she can with an acceptance and a loyalty that the adult reader finds heartbreaking. And therein lies the magic of Gabriella Zalapì's tremendous feat of ventriloquism: Ilaria narrates in the first person, but her voice is devoid of all sentimentality and self-pity, and the author never patronizes her.

In fact, the book is a masterclass of authorial restraint and the art of "show don't tell", and I was at pains to maintain this simplicity. The reader is given information only as and when Ilaria herself assimilates it. We're not told that her father crashes the car: we simply regain consciousness alongside her when she becomes aware of something "grainy and tacky" under her cheek and finds that she hurts all over. This skilful writing means that we often understand things long before Ilaria herself does. For example, we know within only a few pages what her father is doing, but she never truly grasps why she's on this seemingly never-ending peregrination with him. We understand his drinking, his depressive silences, the background music of possible violence, and the shocking way he exploits Ilaria to help with his lost property scam, while she merely describes the facts and her own feelings of discomfort in these circumstances.

Zalapì's restraint is also apparent in the way she handles scenes that other authors might have turned into elaborate set pieces replete with long descriptive passages and swathes of dialogue, such as a trip to a funfair with a nun, and when Ilaria joins in the grape harvest. Ilaria often describes physical sensations but never really tells the reader how she feels about this life, and yet at one point she's so distressed and frustrated by her lack of autonomy that she stops eating. Even here the subject is touched on lightly, seen merely as another episode in a bafflingly nomadic existence, rather than turned into a major theme. One or two other characters simply comment that the child needs a good, square meal.

The book has a strong sense of time and place, with references to real events and extracts of news reports. I wanted to make the journalese of these reports sound very different to the main text, which, despite this sense of time and place, has an elliptical, elusive quality, not unlike a dream. And although it is narrated in the present tense, it feels like something that happened in the past and is not fully remembered or understood, again like a dream. There's nothing whimsical about it, though: Ilaria's loneliness and confusion and her fear of her father's anger are very real. The reader experiences her difficulties along with her and is charmed by her just like the succession of adults who extend their kindness to her along the way.

The quietness and brevity of this book mean that the reader is almost unaware of their own pent-up emotion, and when one of the kindly minor characters gently advises Ilaria's father to do the right thing, the relief packs a remarkable emotional punch. And yet the reader knows—and even Ilaria knows—that her reintegration will be slow and complicated.

Many months after translating the book, this reader often still thinks about Ilaria.

—*Adriana Hunter*

Founded in 2023, Linden Editions is dedicated to publishing outstanding literary works of fiction, narrative non-fiction, reportage and essays. These are primarily in translation, from Europe, the Francophonie and the Mediterranean region.

We live and work internationally and enjoy a mixture of cultures, identities and traditions. We intend to use this access to world literature to discover books that merit international exposure: books which tell compelling stories; books which bring fresh, unforgettable voices; and books which are committed, urgent and challenging.

Linden trees grow all over the world, and are often planted at the centre of village squares. People have been gathering under their shade for generations to share stories. Many cultures see the linden tree as sacred, its perfume all-pervading, and its tea curative. Just like the seeds spread by linden trees, we hope our books will spread the seeds of internationalism further.

To discover more, visit lindeneditions.com.

LINDEN TITLES PUBLISHED AND OUT SOON

Voracious · Małgorzata Lebda
translated from the Polish by Antonia Lloyd-Jones

In Late Summer · Magdalena Blažević
translated from the Croatian by Anđelka Raguž

Struck · Susanna Bissoli
translated from the Italian by Georgia Wall

Not There · Mariusz Szczygieł
translated from the Polish by Antonia Lloyd-Jones

Milk and Blood · Agnès de Clairville
translated from the French by Frank Wynne

My Deformed Body · Egana Djabbarova
translated from the Russian by Lisa C. Hayden